The Fate of
THE BADGER

The Fate of
THE BADGER

Richard Meyer

B T Batsford Ltd London

ISBN 0 7134 51890 (cased)
     0 7134 55047 (limp)

Typeset by S B Datagraphics Ltd, Colchester
and printed in Great Britain by
Anchor-Brendon Ltd
Tiptree, Essex
for the publishers
B. T. Batsford Ltd
4 Fitzhardinge Street
London W1H OAH

Contents

Acknowledgements

Such is the nature of the beast: I am unable to thank by name all those who have helped me produce this book, but they know who they are and they have my deepest respect and gratitude. Theirs is the hardest part to play, and live and die with.

Others balance independence with insecurity – myself included: Special thanks go to many leading members of the BROCK Badger Group in Cornwall – who have had to watch out for the sick and illegal persecution of the badger while forming coherent, sane yet tough opposition to the cool methodology of a state campaign which they believe to be fundamentally flawed and which is exempt from the constraints of law. There is also a heavy road carnage to worry about, and (though not yet in Cornwall) deaths from electrocution by live railway lines.

There are yet others unnamed; they too know who they are: I thank them *for putting up with a tired and distracted friend as I've stolen away to write this book.* Sarah Pym though must be named not just because of her good humour, original ideas and energy but because BROCK, with much help from Kate and Mike Hands (removed to an academic set in Cambridge), grew out of her old Cornwall Badger Protection League. I owe much to her early spade work (if I can use that expression in this context). Not only that but I parasitized shamelessly some of her research.

While I wrote I was being supported by a research grant from the World Wildlife Fund – who are keen to establish liaison links between affected and interested parties in the troubled South-West so that the persecution of the badger may be minimised and kept within the bounds of the law. My deep thanks, therefore, to WWF and particularly Mark Carwardine and Craig Johnson for their understanding interest and support in a difficult job. Also my thanks to the Wildlife Link Badger Working Group for their splendid October 1984 Report to Professor Dunnet's Review Team, which has almost become a bible on the complex problem of badgers and tuberculosis.

I also want to thank John Bainbridge and the Dartmoor Badgers Protection League, Dr Paul Barrow, Ian Beales (of the Bristol United

Press), Dr Chris Cheeseman (and his staff in MAFF's Gloucestershire ecological study which promises so much for objective science), David Coffey, Nick Couldrey (of the League Against Cruel Sports), Tony Crittenden, Phil Drabble, James Henderson (of Express Newspapers), Gill Hunt, Lyn Jenkins, John Kennet, Adrian Langdon, Dr David Macdonald, Dr Kahlid Mahmood, Graham Ovenden, Eunice Overend, David Penhaligon MP, Sue and David Philp, Dr Derek Pout, E Jane Ratcliffe, Professor Eric Robinson, holder of the copyright on John Clare's poems, for his contribution (see Appendix VI), Dr John Stanford, Elizabeth Stevens (of the Curtis Brown Group) and Michele Vaughan who have all helped in special ways. Also thanks to my friends in the Ministry, and for MAFF's civility in always doing their best to answer my many questions. I acknowledge the difficulty of the position they now find themselves in.

My sincere thanks to Robin Hanbury-Tenison – farmer, conservationist and explorer – who has seen the effects of 'the white man's plague' in other guises and in other farther-flung places, and who normally works for oppressed minorities even less able to withstand the conceit and galloping consumption of modern man. I would like to leave the last words for Dr Ernest Neal and Eric Ashby, to thank them on behalf of all naturalists for the interest their work spawned. In my case it implanted after about six years but thereafter grew steadily on such rich nutrition.

The author and publishers would like to thank the following for kind permission to reproduce black and white photographs:

Dartmoor Badgers Protection League (1, 2, 9)
League against Cruel Sports (3, 4a, 4b, 5b, 5)
Lancashire Evening Post (4c, 4d, 4e, 4f)
Gwent Badger Group (5)
Adrian Langdon (6, 7, 8, 11, 12, 16)
Graham Ovenden (17)
Middlesex Hospital and Visual Arts TV Ltd (inset in 12)
and the following for kind permission to reproduce illustrations:
Curtis Brown Ltd, London (Fig 1 – illustration by E H Shepard copyright under the Berne Convention)
Express Newspapers plc (Figs 2 and 3)
New Scientist (Fig 5 – prepared by Dr Paul Barrow)
Blackwell Scientific Publications Ltd (Fig 6)
The Veterinary Record (Figs 7a and 7b)
Frederick Warne (Publishers) (Fig 4)

R.M.M.
Hellandbridge, Cornwall
July 1985

Foreword

I have lived and farmed cattle and sheep on Bodmin Moor for over 25 years. There are a lot of badgers on my farm and I enjoy their presence. I like meeting them in the lanes at night and, on occasion, watching them as they forage unaware in the evening.

At the same time, I am aware that tuberculin tests have been a regular feature of farming life over the years; all the cattle have to be rounded up and penned, 'doubtful' reactors causing tiresome delays when stock may not be taken to market. It would be good if the disease could be 'eradicated', but the pressure from farmers has not been intense while compensation for compulsorily slaughtered animals is available.

Then one day I found a very sick badger on the road near the farmhouse. It was clearly dying and in distress so I put it out of its misery. It was so wasted I could lift it between finger and thumb. What next? If I contacted the Ministry and they found it had TB then our cattle would be tested and if a reactor was found all the badgers on the farm might be killed. I knew that this policy was highly questionable and I resolved to fight it if I had to. But I still contacted the Ministry because not to have done so would have been immoral and would simply have postponed the issue. The Ministry vet who arrived to collect the badger said it had probably died of TB. Several months later I heard that the tests had proved negative.

When I first met Richard Meyer I told him this story and said how disturbed I was about being ill-informed on the subject. If I was ever going to have to defend the badgers on my land, I wanted to know the facts. 'Someone should write a book about it all' I said. 'I am doing' he replied, and also told me that he was working for the World Wildlife Fund on the problem of bovine TB in badgers. Since then, he has visited the farm several times and we have walked the woods and hedgerows in search of badger sets. It has been a revelation to me and a humbling experience to discover that I share this land with so many of these fine and fascinating animals. I am also more than ever convinced that the Ministry's policy is wrong, inhumane and ill-founded; and I believe that anyone who reads this book will find it hard to disagree.

Tuberculosis is today almost a myth disease in Europe. The 'galloping consumption' which carried off our ancestors no longer exists here and deaths from bovine TB are extremely rare. It is also increasingly recognised that stress plays a major role. I have seen this often for myself among the tribal peoples whom I have visited in South-East Asia and South America. When a small tribe of Amazonian Indians is forcibly 'translocated' to a new and unfamiliar territory, TB is almost sure to follow as their physical and psychological health deteriorates. It seems the same may be true of badgers. It is ironic, therefore, that efforts to eradicate the disease may actually make things worse.

The economics of this policy appear ludicrous, even in the crazy world of official agricultural costings today. With a conservative estimate of £2 million being spent on badger control in the South-West, ample compensation could be paid to farmers for reactors while research could be undertaken into oral vaccines and other methods of combatting this relatively minor disease.

While considering the fate of the badger, Richard Meyer makes us look at ourselves. Without sentiment or bitterness he exposes us as a species of dubious worth. Most of us like badgers instinctively. It is shocking to learn how cruelly they are still being slaughtered, not so much for sport now as in the name of official government policy. We are appalled at the prospect of living in a land from which they have been totally exterminated. This book makes us understand why the controversy is so important; why much more than the fate of the badger alone is involved.

Robin Hanbury-Tenison

Prelude

'It's the nearest thing we've got to a proper animal!'

I think I knew what she meant.

'Other countries have lions, bears and pandas; what have we got?' She answered her own question. 'A fox that's protected so it can be hunted, an otter that's about had it, and a wildcat that no-one ever sees.'

She was talking, of course, about British carnivores. It seemed churlish to mention seals – good marine carnivores – and those much smaller relatives of the badger's, the stoat and weasel. She probably wouldn't have been much impressed anyway. The pine marten? That's about as rare as the otter.

'They're not going to kill them all,' I ventured.

'Maybe not, but they're having a bloody good go...anyway, what about the passenger pigeon?'

I thought about this bird that had once blackened the skies over America with its countless millions, and yet had been piecemeal blasted to extinction just because no-one cared until too late.

'That couldn't happen now,' I said without conviction.

'Maybe not,' she said again, equally unconvinced.

I remained quiet, unsure of what to say next. I understood exactly her fears, and she sensed my unease.

'What is it about the badger anyway?' she challenged.

This book, I suppose, is an attempt at an answer.

Introduction

'The Last Proper Animal'

When midnight comes...

(Clare)

We have, in our juvenile emergence from some primeval soup, travelled far from the shores of a natural state, and penetrated the deep hinterland of the mind. Our image is in love with itself. And we have allocated ourselves alone a soul and a spirit. But are we a part of creation or the Creator?

Man has fabricated a world of illusion and self-deception for so long that he now truly believes he has dominion. The world exists for him: its precious treasures are his to squander; its land his to appropriate; its wild inhabitants his to manipulate, control, exploit and, if the whim takes him, destroy. Because its other life-forms cannot speak his language, he assumes they have no soul. But if a cow could talk, would the slaughterman hesitate..? Maybe he would hesitate for ever.

Do animals not speak? If not, why do they listen; why do they observe. Why do we try to understand? Life speaks – all organic matter speaks: one day this will not seem strange. Self-infatuation elevates and detaches; and it grows on a culture of affluence. It is, therefore, most manifest in what we appropriate as the Developed World. It is here, or in its name, that we defile beauty and call it progress.

Britain illustrates well: small, compact and yet astonishingly complex. It is, or rather was, an exquisite trove of natural and archaeological treasure. This has to a large extent gone or been deformed beyond recognition; what remains is at the mercy of man; nothing is really safe. We live in a contrived world, taking what we want and sanctioning the rest. Yet something remains. And the badger is symbolic to many of the spirit of vestigial British wilderness.

Why is the badger more symbolic than anything else? If we can discover this perhaps we will understand better.

Apart from the few stretches of unspoiled wilderness left in Britain there is no widespread topographical link with our past remaining:

most inches of our landscape are manscape now. It cannot be plant life because that is prey to both insidious and catastrophic land change; so it must be animal and it must be of a size and a character that we can appreciate. The poor woodlouse hardly scores. Birds? Too mobile, too transient – those that remain are either too man-orientated or too remote.

The human looks to another mammal. The large animal no longer occurs on British land unless sanctioned. It has not, in fact, for many centuries. Seals are marine, their world alien. Our native deer are condoned or managed because they serve us well; and only the red deer is large. Would the fox have gone the way of the wolf were it not for the perversities of the pleasure-hunter, who protects to pursue, and proclaims a civil liberty? From most of these pages the fox, the warm and sultry fox, must watch from the shadows.

What on British earth is left besides the badger? As my saddened girl declared, only a cat and an otter that few can ever see, and which have been forced to the farthest reaches. The Scottish wildcat is closer to my heart than even the badger, but fate has decreed that I live for the present in Cornwall – as far away on common ground from my beloved wildcat as I could possibly be. So now that I can no longer have the wildcat for my neighbour, the badger has crept into its place.

Of the two, the badger at least deserves our respect. If ever Britain wants an emblematic animal more appropriate to its homely size, influence and geographical position, now that the grand and empirical lion seems increasingly absurd and outrageous, the badger, if there's any justice, must have a bye to the final.

So, what is it about the badger? Where does it lie now this 'most ancient Briton of English beasts' as the poet Edward Thomas called him?

For Sarah

(*And brocks everywhere*)

The dropping wind seemed whispering in affright
As if it felt the presence of midnight
While passing through the dismal deepening woods
Buried in night and awful solitudes

'Badger Catchers' – John Clare (1793–1864)

ONE

Alas, Poor Brock

...a host of dogs and men

(Clare)

'One of the most inoffensive animals inhabiting this planet,' a journalist once wrote about the badger. I would agree, and only graft in the word 'wild' before animal.

There has never been a British animal more unjustly abused than the badger yet there has never been one more cherished by children, or more admired by the reasonable and sane. Through absolutely no fault of its own, the badger has been shunned, feared, maligned, attacked, tortured and victimised. Now, additionally, it appears snared on the coat-tails of bureaucracy. And yet it has survived so far; many others haven't. Like the model silent hero, it is also strong and shy and runs the risk of being misunderstood and persecuted. Its shyness is seen as weakness, its silence as insolence; that character, together with the handsome bold appearance of the badger challenges the barbaric heart of man.

Tragically, even the scientist, given incentive, can mis-read his data, and believe that perception is truth. The badger, as we shall see, can still appear today as much a convenient diversion as it was to the medieval sorcerer.

'To badger', as everyone knows, means relentless persecution. Words may enter our language on a whim as 'vogue words' but they do not become assimilated on one, nor do they lose their self-consciousness without good trial. For 'badgering' to have attained its current prevalence, original exposure must have been widespread and appropriate. Some believe that 'badger' has derived from the French word *becheur* meaning 'a digger', although in English the white blaze (badge) has certainly played a large part in its relatively recent etymology (badge-ard = white forehead). Prior to the mid-eighteenth century, the names 'brock' (in various forms), 'bawson', 'grey' and 'pate' were commonly used. Of these, only 'brock' is now frequent.

'Brock' returns us to the Old Celtic 'broc' meaning grey or grizzled – which is apt enough description of the badger's colouration, and this, judging by the number of place-names beginning with it was by far the most common – even in Wales, where *mochyn daear* (pig of the forest) is now preferred by the purist. In Eire, the badger is still sometimes referred to as the 'earth pig'.

Villages or towns named, I assume, after the badger are Brockdam in Northumberland, Brockdish on the River Waveney in Suffolk and its neighbour Brockford Green, Brockenhurst in the New Forest, Brockhall near Watling Street in Northants, Brockham near Boxhill in Surrey, two Brockhamptons – one in the Cotswolds, and one over the Severn near Hereford, Brockholes near Huddersfield (an obvious reference to a large set or sets), there is a Brockhurst near Portsmouth and one in Warwickshire, Brocklebank in Cumbria, Brocklesby in north Lincolnshire, Brockley near Bristol, Brockley Green south of Bury St Edmunds, there are no fewer than four Brocktons in Shropshire, a Brockweir near Tintern Abbey in the Forest of Dean, a Brockwell north of Chepstow, and Brockworth near Gloucester.

In addition 'Brock' is often shortened to 'Broc', and 'Brocks' to 'Brox'. There are many Broctons, including one in Cannock Chase. Amongst places with the prefix 'Brox-', there are Broxa in North Yorkshire, indeed a Broxa Forest, Broxbourne north of London, two Broxburns south of the Firth of Forth in Scotland, Broxholme near Lincoln, Broxstowe in Nottingham, Broxted near Bishop's Stortford, Broxton near the Welsh border in Cheshire, and Broxwood in west Herefordshire.

Fig 1 'When all was quite ready, the Badger took a dark lantern in one paw, grasped his great stick with the other and said, "Now then, follow me!"' Badger and his friends prepare for their battle with the weasels at the end of *The Wind in the Willows*. (*Illustration by E H Shepard, copyright under the Berne Convention, reproduced by permission of Curtis Brown Ltd, London*)

There are many more: in Cornwall there is Brocks, Brocken Burrow, Brochill and Brocton. And, of course, there are, in addition, several place names in which the word appears as a suffix. Very close to my home, for instance, is Polbrock – which means 'the badgers' pool'. Elsewhere in Cornwall, there is Polbroke from the same stem.

Surely some of these names reflect affection or at least amused interest rather than fear, hatred and suspicion. On a more local level, innumerable farms, fields, woods and landmarks bear witness. Ritson Graham in his article *The Badger in Cumberland* written in 1946 says

The familiar place name of *brock* alone ranges the country from the lower reaches of the River Eden to a number of crags extending up to two thousand feet...whilst the many farms, field and fell names of which Brocklewath, Brockholes, Brocklands and Brocklebank are typical examples, all testify to the prevalence and wide distribution of the badger in former times.

The name 'bawson' derives from 'bausoned' meaning white-spotted or striped. 'Pate' of course refers to the badger's 'bald' or white crown. It is largely a northern term, and in Durham there is a glen called Pate-priest's Glen apparently after a priest who lived there as a hermit and hunted badgers. And in the West Riding of Yorkshire there is a Pateley Bridge near, incidentally, a Greygarth. There seems little doubt that some of the place-names prefixed with 'Grey-' refer to the badger; one which is definitely thought to is Greywell in Hampshire.

The badger has probably tenanted the British Isles for at least the last 400,000 years in a virtually unchanged form. Fossil records go back approximately 250,000 years but in Europe they have been found in early Pleistocene deposits – over a million years old – virtually indistinguishable from today's animal. The original type is thought to be three million years old.

He has withstood much since man arrived in his world but the ignorant and random brutality of our ancestors is *not* to be compared to the might of a Government department keen to manage nature. Of this, much more later, but it is relevant here to record that despite civilisation, the rise of rational science, and we like to think humanity, man is still capable of acts of cool genocide against bystanders. It is a classic quirk of irony that during the dawn of official protection – granted the badger in 1973 – a mighty onslaught was officially launched. Nobody knows how many badgers were gassed but it was probably about 15,000 before the practice was replaced by shooting.

The policy, after initial puzzlement, was seen as a nod and wink by the rural louts. So much so that the illegal persecution of badgers even began to exceed the level during the sixties, when it had come to be seen as the outdated perversion of a few sad relics.

The Badgers Act 1973 was designed to mop up these throwbacks and squeeze them into the twentieth century but it could not cope with the incitement suddenly presented to the British straw-dogs, who saw a chance to sate their sadism and bloodlust, flout authority and outrage public concern all at the same time.

The badger was once again fair game: it was there but self-effacing, it possessed all the qualities which bullies the world over seek out and exploit: the popular hero, strong and silent. In a way it became a kind of real life Robert Mitchum, a butt for the drunken rowdy. To channel cruelty through a third party, thus saving any risk to oneself, is a good cowardly tactic; so dogs, terriers mostly, come to do man's dirty work; in the process they are themselves perverted. At least the bar-room bore picks his own fight.

Dogs are central to the history of man versus wild animal. They have been domesticated since at least Mesolithic times, i.e. before the development of cultivation in Neolithic times, and domesticated of course means manipulated – trained and bred either to do the things man cannot or will not do himself or to become an extension of his own personality. Of the many functions of different breeds of dogs, the fierce or aggressive one extends the power and influence of his master: it will, of course, fight his fights, and divert unwanted attention.

I have little doubt that primitive man lived harmoniously with his wild animal brethren – that is not to say peacefully – but hunting them when forced to do so through self-defence or hunger, otherwise avoiding and observing them. Just when the badger's unreasoned persecution began, I cannot say. They were eaten, and still are in places; badger 'hams' – the hind flanks, salted and smoked – are reputed to be excellent, tasting like fine pork. Maybe raw it is not so good, for even the fox is said to refuse badger meat.

So badgers were eaten when they could be caught, and were likely considered a feast; indeed, an annual badger feast continued until recently at a public house near Yeovil in Somerset, with the hams being roasted over an open fire. Their pelts and fur have also been put to several uses; on account of their coarseness they were not much used for coats but made high quality footwear: according to *Ezekiel* XVI, 10, prosperous Israelites were 'clothed in fine linen and shod with badgers' skins'. Such durability was also put to good use much later, and badger pelts are used in the Caucasus and Siberia for pistol holsters, and in Scotland for sporrans. The Royal Argyll and Sutherland Highlanders now use a synthetic substitute but there are still genuine articles in service, now of an antique vintage. A badger trapper in Scotland was called a '*brochen*'.

Alongside these more mundane uses for animal products, badgers also yielded a wide range of lotions and potions as dark and mysterious as the animal itself – properties which Gerard would no doubt have called 'vertues'. It is not really surprising, given the badger's nocturnal wanderings; its woodland, subterranean chambers; its retiring habits (some would say furtive) and occasional eerie shrieks, that it became an expeditious and convenient villain by which to diffuse the irrational fears which trouble uneducated folk living close to nature, and to explain away the otherwise inexplicable.

Witches either had or pretended to have superior senses, and this supernatural affinity they externalised by employing whatever beasts, plants and other natural phenomena suited their purpose. Their power and influence were thus furthered and they were able to sublimate themselves as interpreters rather than causal agents.

To this end, the badger must have been invaluable. Not only was it reasonably large by British standards and of striking appearance but it also had a suitable shadowy image. It came to be seen as a threat.

Knowing what we know now about its biology, it is difficult to understand this irrational fear until we stop to contemplate the fate of all Britain's large wild animals. Man has long regarded as a threat or

Fig 2 Rupert's chum, Bill Badger, has aged little in the nearly thirty years that separate figs 2 and 3, illustrations by Alfred Bestall. In *Rupert's Who's Who* (1984) Bill is described as 'A very close pal. Easygoing. Can take a joke. Useful in a tight spot. Always looks on the bright side. One of Rupert's oldest friends.'

challenge (the two words as nouns are virtually synonymous anyway) any natural event that is perceived to be out of control. Today this can be seen applied to any area of so-called wasteland, even an old tree or unkempt hedge.

A ransom was placed on its head. Ritson Graham researched parish registers in the Lake District and discovered that for nearly a century, from 1658 to 1741 (the earliest and latest dates found, from Penrith and Ulverston respectively) the payment ranged from fourpence to one shilling per head. Other parishes involved in this bounty-hunting were Kendal, Kirby Londsdale and Orton; Kendal paid out for 73 heads in one eight-year period.

Such an attitude does not seem to have prevailed on the continent, though this needs researching more thoroughly. In Germany, Vogt in his *Mammalia* of 1887 describes much more accurately a gentle and domestic beast who only becomes fierce if alarmed or threatened. He was considered the protector and brother of the fox, and fable has it

Fig 3 'Bill likes the idea and so the two pals move off quickly, taking care not to be seen.' From *Rupert and the Black Circle*. (*Illustrations for Rupert Stories by courtesy and kind permission of Express Newspapers plc*)

that he constantly endeavoured, despite Reynard's trickery, to lead the fox back to the path of virtue. We can, incidentally, see from this that the British stereotyped image of the fox is *not* so different from that demonstrated on mainland Europe.

I have used the central verses of a moving but untitled poem of John Clare's to lead off each chapter because it illustrates so well the lone voice of the visionary; it may be found in its entirety at the end of the book. The badger has impressed other writers too apart from ploughman poets such as Clare and Edward Thomas, but in *The Life and Habits of the Badger* published in 1914, J Fairfax-Blakeborough and A E Pease collect several interesting pieces which only go to show how effective the anti-badger propaganda had been.

Dr Ernest Neal in his revolutionary monograph of 1948 towards the end hopes

as people come to know more about these grand animals they will revise their opinions, based on stupidity and ignorance, and begin to appreciate the presence of one of the finest animals on our fauna list.

No-one has done more to help achieve this than Neal himself, and no-one can now hope to write or think about badgers without referring constantly to him. I am no exception, and I am extremely grateful to him for giving me permission to quote from his great writings on the subject. And shamelessly I must begin, for it was in Dr Neal's *The Badger* that I first found the Fairfax-Blakeborough reference to a manuscript compiled by David Naitby in about 1800:

> Should one hear a badger call,
> And then an ullot [owl] cry,
> Make thy peace with God, good soul,
> For shortly thou shalt die.

One Mistress Braithwaite is believed to have written the following in her 'well-thumbed copy of Holy Writ':

> Should a badger cross the path
> Which thou hast taken, then
> Good luck is thine, so it be said
> Beyond the luck of men.
> But if it cross in front of thee,
> Beyond where thou shalt tread,
> And if by chance doth turn the mould,
> Thou art numbered with the dead.

The powers of the badger are evidently profuse. And there seems to have been an upsurge of interest in it at the turn of the seventeenth century, for in the the *Sporting Magazine* in 1800, the following, again after Neal, is printed:

The flesh, blood and grease of the badger are very useful for oils, ointments, salves and powders, for shortness of breath, the cough of the lungs [*more than a little ironic today*] for the stone, sprained sinews, collachs etc. The skin being well dressed is very warm and comfortable for ancient people who are troubled with paralytic disorders.

Again from David Naitby's collection comes the following:

A tuft of hair gotten from the head of a full-grown Brock is powerful to ward off all manner of witchcraft; these must be worn in a little bag made of cat's skin – a black cat – and tied about the neck when the moon be not more than seven days old, and under that aspect when the planet Jupiter be mid-heaven at midnight.

No doubting the pedigree of this!

As Ernest Neal points out: 'The merits of badger grease are upheld by many an old countryman'. As recently as the last war it was sold without difficulty by an old villager near Cheltenham; people apparently coming long distances to procure it. It is still considered a good embrocation, especially for horses.

Much earlier references are to be found in the Old Testament. Apart from the application of badger skins for footwear alluded to in *Ezekiel*, tabernacles were to be covered with 'rams' skins dyed red, and above badgers' skins' (*Exodus* XXVI, 14).

A Victorian naturalist described the badger as

An animal of considerable strength of character and individual charm and though its little peccadilloes may bring it into conflict with either the farmer or the game preserver, few animals of its size can boast so shameless a life.

Nothing much has changed, though as a threat to game the badger is now considered, even by most gamekeepers, as inconsequential.

In the past, gamekeepers could not of course have been expected to turn a blind eye to the badger, and Phil Drabble in his book *No Badgers In My Wood* graphically recalls the hard line that used to prevail.

Fig 4 'Now Tommy Brock did occasionally eat rabbit-pie; but it was only very little young ones occasionally, when other food was really scarce. He was friendly with old Mr Bouncer . . .' Tommy Brock was 'passing through the wood with a sack and a little spade which he used for digging, and some mole traps' before his adventure with Mr Tod in Beatrix Potter *The Tale of Mr Tod*.

Gamekeepers never showed much interest in objective natural history, only in amassing evidence, however tenuous, to justify the eradication of anything which could conceivably be seen as a threat to their enjoyment and prospects. The most extensive persecution of this kind was during the nineteenth century – the heyday of the great game estates. Until World War II, when most gamekeepers went off to fight a rather more dangerous enemy, huntsmen in particular liked a few badgers around so that they could be blamed for the fox's misdeeds.

Even now there are all sorts of countrymen who endeavour to disguise their own inadequacies by passing the buck to wildlife, and the badger does not escape despite its diet — largely beneficial to man — and a surprisingly low profile.

But generally, today, the badger's enemies are to be found at opposite ends of the legal spectrum. Farmers, as managers of the vast majority of the countryside, sometimes find an enemy where they are not looking for one, and themselves in a difficult position. There are a few who regard badgers and wildlife in general as their personal burden but increasingly they are prepared to 'farm round 'em', as one Cornish farmer put it when contemplating a huge set in the middle of a field.

However, the badger, along with other wildlife, is still used and abused in a way that wouldn't be tolerated were the animal a dog, cat or horse. Whether badger hair shaving brushes are better or worse than those made of synthetic filaments, I really cannot say. A spokesman for *Boots*, the chemists, in defence of their exploitation of the wild badger said in 1980 that

British badgers do not produce hair suitable for the brush trade and *it is not used for any type of brush*. The most suitable badger hair is imported from China in particular, also from the Balkan countries, where climatic conditions enable the badger to flourish.

Pressed again the following year, he said:

The British manufacturers of badger shaving brushes have to be sure of a regular supply of suitable badger hair and this is imported. Not only is the imported badger hair more suitable, but the continuity of supply is imperative. The manufacturers cannot rely on picking up the odd badger pelt in the UK.

A report in *Oryx* in January 1972 revealed that the newest threat then to the badger was the demand from fashion houses for its fur in trimming hats.

There is one predator, rather less genteel, which dwarfs the combined efforts of the evilly disposed digger, baiter, snarer, trapper (whether in Eastern Europe or elsewhere), gamekeeper and, it is suggested, though during the gloomy years of mass gassing this seemed unlikely, the Ministry of Agriculture. This supreme predator is also the most wasteful; it is, of course, the motor vehicle.

It will be noted that all these predators are man in one guise or another. The badger has no other enemy. But maybe one is enough.

TWO

The Killer Disease

He turns about to face the loud uproar

(Clare)

Just the word 'tuberculosis' (TB) is capable of inspiring fear, and not just to dairy farmers and chest physicians. The disease is still little understood, indeed it may never be fully understood for it was declining in humans even before it was discovered to be caused by bacteria. All the indications are that tuberculosis declines naturally when faced with increased living standards. Nevertheless, there are various strains of TB; the human type was, and still is in some parts of the world, a real scourge. Typically it appears in stressful over-crowded conditions, and can thus be regarded as one of nature's ways of limiting over-population. So when we fight it directly we are taking on a natural phenomenon. It is perhaps best combatted by avoiding the conditions in which it works.

An encyclopaedia from 1969 picked out at random contains the following description:

No disease causes more public concern, nor is more difficult to describe; for the tubercle germ can attack many different parts of the body and manifest itself in many ways... The bacillus is particularly hardy, so that when coughed or spat out on the ground it continues to be infectious for a long time... But there is a good deal more to the problem than this; we know, for example, that over 90 per cent of people in industrialised countries have been infected with TB in early life and have conquered the infection...

History is pock-marked by the disease, or 'galloping consumption' as it was often called. In some areas members from every other family along streets were taken by it. It was no respecter of eminence, wealth, fame or even location once exposed to it. Robert Louis Stevenson succumbed on a Pacific Island, the Brontës in the Yorkshire countryside, Chopin in France, St Teresa in a convent, D H Lawrence on his return to England from foreign travels. Other exotic victims were Aubrey Beardsley, Franz Kafka and Napoleon II.

Jilted Victorian lovers traditionally went into a decline and died of a 'broken heart'; TB, induced or aggravated by emotional stress was usually, unromantically, the culprit. The frozen hand of Mimi immortalised by Puccini is a classic example.

The most severe forms of poor, overcrowded living conditions and malnutrition have been abolished in Britain, and this has removed the source of much infectious disease. Spitting, once common in public places, is now socially unacceptable, and *Spitting Prohibited* signs have become as rare as the disease they were designed to help control. Dogs – highly susceptible to TB – were likely to lick at infected spittal and become an obvious carrier between separate human populations.

Human TB still afflicts people living in sub-standard conditions but in Britain it is now only a real problem in immigrant communities. Not just because such communities may bring the disease in with them and often congregate in crowded conditions but also because of the debilitating effects of emotional and physical stress. As anyone knows who has ever removed – let alone emigrated to another country, climate and culture – the strain of moving house is not so dissimilar to that affecting a jilted lover.

Why should the same syndrome not exist with other variations of the disease in other life-forms? Human beings cherish the notion that they alone feel such ordeals deeply. Farmers who prefer not to use markets, and only extremely rarely buy or sell stock direct to another farm evidently feel for their animals, and experience their anxieties as parents do their children's. They confirm that a cow moved to a new home loses its friends, its social position and all the landmarks which give it security. A cow does not decide to move and is unable to comprehend this colossal upheaval in its life; it is adversely and seriously affected for months. Scientific experiments back this observation.

The TB strain that is serious in cattle is *Mycobacterium bovis*, also called the bovine tubercle bacillus (bovine TB). Recent work suggests that human, bovine and murine (rodent) types are so closely related that Dr John Grange in 1982, in a reappraisal of the disease one hundred years after it was first identified by Robert Koch, recommends the term *M. tuberculosis* for all, with the cattle disease, for example, having the suffix 'bovine type bacilli'.

Much of the earlier debate is discussed in a major review by the same worker with C H Collins one year later. Koch blundered in claiming 'the human subject is immune against infection with bovine bacilli and is so slightly susceptible that it is not necessary to take any steps to counteract risk of infection'. Although most experts disagreed, his brilliant reputation meant that his belief had far-reaching effects. Some scientists continue to feel that by exonerating cows from any involvement in human incidence, Koch put back the clock of veterinary preventive medicine to a much greater degree than is generally accepted.

A Royal Commission was appointed in 1901 to resolve the controversy. It deliberated for ten years and established three important principles: i) there were three types of pathogenic tubercle bacilli (human, bovine and avian) as well as saprophytic mycobacteria; ii) pulmonary (lung) TB in humans could be contracted by inhaling the bovine bacilli; and iii) bovine TB in cows' milk caused alimentary TB in humans. The Royal Commission concluded that tuberculous cattle were a direct hazard to human health. It was instrumental in promoting veterinary tuberculin testing (see Appendix I), which was to have such a significant effect on a disease that was at that time claiming over 2,000 humans deaths a year quite apart from the many thousands dying of human TB.

It should not be surprising, considering successive governments' reluctance to take our environment seriously, that it was not until 1935 – some 25 years after the Royal Commission – that the Ministry of Agriculture's voluntary Attested Herds Scheme was introduced, the ultimate aim being to *eradicate* the disease. The USA began their eradication programme in 1917, and still have outbreaks.

Let us, just for a moment, consider this word 'eradicate' because it crops up continually in this story. It is a worrying word for it is symptomatic of an attitude which is ruthless and unimaginative. No doubt bureaucracies the world over need absolutes, around which red tape strangles instead of holding together. Absolutes beget hosts of regulations which defy life; they ignore the fundamental virtue in any dynamic system – variability. We vary, therefore all life is dynamic. Absolutes like 'eradicate' attempt to be self-existent but reveal tyranny. With disease, such a policy is dangerous. The lessons of malaria exist to teach us that. Bacteria can reproduce every 25 minutes, a super strain is a horrifying prospect. A rash onslaught on a docile low level in equilibrium could be a little like taking a 5lb hammer to the last remaining vial of smallpox.

Much later, when the incidence of bovine TB in cattle had been brought down to an extremely low level – well under one per cent – there was a good opportunity to reconsider the situation. Had good sense and a sensitivity to ecological forces prevailed, officials would have done well to wait and watch. But it was not to be.

'Eradicate' is a big word; perhaps we are not yet big enough to appreciate fully its implications.

The single-minded drive to eradicate a mycobacterium in cattle was no doubt born out of political hyperbole and a genuine concern for public health. Now to perpetuate it could well be foolhardy and irrational – especially while we acknowledge a small but diverse reservoir elsewhere in the environment. Idealism corrupts realism; in this case it obscures the great work done by many vets in the early days of the disease control campaign.

Now we must have total control. Twenty-five years was a long time to make a decision but the prospect was daunting. In the 1930's, about 40% of all cattle slaughtered in public abattoirs had *obvious* tubercular lesions. It was agreed in 1934 that *at least* 40% of cows in dairy herds were also infected. By the end of 1935, 22,237 cattle had reacted to the tuberculin test and been slaughtered, and yet this accounted for less than one hundred herds. Three years later, there were 4,644 'clean' herds. But then came World War II, and the scheme – still voluntary but with inducements – was shelved. It was resumed after the war in 1945, and made compulsory in 1950 on an area-by-area plan. For some bureaucratic reason, the scheme began in Scotland and worked steadily south, this had the effect of sweeping infected cattle down towards the south-west. Ten years later, by 1960, all herds had been tested, and in 1961 the annual test reactor rate was 0.16%, and only 3.5% of herds contained infected animals. Another five years and the figures had been reduced to 0.05% and 1.0% respectively. By 1979, except in the south-west the reactor rate was about 0.01% and only 0.18% of herds were infected. It has been suggested by Grange and Collins that this may represent an irreducible minimum.

Whether it does or not, it was a remarkable achievement, and the result of a bold and sensitive scheme; essentially it was one which was under control and coincided with a general improvement in standards. The current policy has been likened to a mopping-up operation, but after ten years, the reactor incidence has declined by only about 0.03%; during this time attention has been focussed on the badger almost exclusively.

The World of the Giant Killer Cell

Is it possible to comprehend this disease without a training in microbiology? Given an interest in life, I believe, yes, for scale is all that conceals. With an effort we can comprehend the minutiae, and once across the size barrier we notice that life follows similar principles. It is important to persevere with this because one of the main hopes for the badger in south-west England (a remaining stronghold), if government action against them continues, lies in understanding its immune system.

Bacteria are microscopic organisms – often they are regarded as the most primitive group of plants. We need help to see them because they are amongst the smallest of all known single-celled organisms. Most are shaped as rods, and they range in size from 1/50000 to 1/5000 of an inch. They vary in breadth mostly from 0.5 to 2.0 microns. It has been calculated that 250,000 bacteria could 'sit' on the full stop at the end of this sentence. There are uncountable millions in the environment: a gram of soil can contain several thousand or several hundred millions. Here they do a vital job in the carbon and nitrogen cycles – breaking down plant and animal tissues, liberating food for higher plants. They also make available organic compounds by converting them to inorganic nitrogen compounds (nitrates). Bacteria can reproduce outside a living body, rapidly and repeatedly dividing in two.

However, comprehending is not understanding. Tuberculosis – the disease prompted by the tubercle, which is the manifestation of the organism – is not fully understood even by specialists. Its world is a sub-world, a world within a world. Every living thing with a vascular system is a planet to a bacterium. Our eco-system is their outer space; each being representing a world or a planet.

Bacteria, judging by distribution and numbers, are the most successful of life-forms; they occupy every aerobic and anaerobic environment where energy supplying substrates are to be found. Only very few cause disease, and it is quite wrong to think of them as undesirable; for theirs is a world with baddies and goodies too.

When our body's first defences – the mechanical barriers such as the skin and mucous membranes – are breached by invading pathogenic bacteria, the second line of defence is triggered: the phagocytes. These represent the *innate, non-specific immune response*. Phagocytes are white blood cells, specialised as killer cells; when alerted chemically, they move towards the invading micro-organisms (the bacilli), bind with them, then engulf and digest them. Most bacteria are digested within two hours but organisms such as *M. tuberculosis* are pathogenic because of their special ability to resist enzyme destruction by such phagocytes.

After intra-cellular (inside the cells) growth of the bacteria, the phagocytes become laden with the bacilli, die, disintegrate and then release the bacilli which become engulfed by further cells or disseminated throughout the body. Multiplication often occurs extra-cellularly (outside the cells) before the bacilli are re-ingested. If all the bacilli are destroyed by phagocytosis, the disease is defeated.

There is a third line of defence waiting for bacilli which avoid or survive phagocytosis – this is called the *acquired, specific immune response*. The effectiveness of this response depends on the age and environmental experience of the animal. There are two closely related forms. One is effected by large antibodies (the *humoral* immune response) produced from B-lymphocyte cells – often shortened to B-cells. Lymphocytes are a bit like a vigilante patrol – they circulate in the blood and lymphatic system (a system of blind-ended fluid-containing tubes which permeate the body, and which join larger capillaries, and finally the venous system near the heart). They derive from cells originating in the bone marrow. Once processed by the bone marrow (B-lymphocytes) and thymus (T-lymphocytes), they become what is called *immunocompetent* in the spleen and lymphodes.

On stimulation by an invading antigen (from a particular invading micro-organism), B-cells capable of recognising that specific antigen begin to mobilise: multiplying and differentiating.

Thus a group of specifically committed antibody-secreting B-lymphocytes is produced which coats invading bacilli with specific antibodies which in turn ensure that they are specifically recognised by the body's phagocytes. They also neutralise toxins produced by the invader, and thus help the innate response.

It is important to remember that we are not born with this specific immune ability. It is only acquired after challenge from the antigen(s) of invading micro-organisms. The response is then *specific* to the antigen(s). This way immunity develops as exposure to invaders increases.

The same goes for the second form of specific response – cell-mediated immunity (CMI). This involves the thymus processed cells – the T-lymphocytes. They lodge in particular areas of the spleen and lymph-nodes.

In bacterial disease such as tuberculosis and brucellosis, it is felt that the B-cells are unable to control the disease by themselves – but they may well help in T-lymphocyte transformation. This occurs when an invading antigen stimulates the T-cells to multiply and differentiate into an activated force – known as lymphocyte transformation.

The T-cells are then sensitised and antigen-specific. They produce a number of non-antibody lymphocytic factors known collectively as lymphokines. In the typical mammalian host they are probably responsible for the following defensive actions:

i) the production of modified T-lymphocytes known as 'killer cells' which accumulate at the site of infection and destroy invading micro-organisms;

ii) further stimulation and proliferation of normal, unsensitised T-lymphocytes;

iii) the chemotactic (that is, in response to chemical stimulus) attraction of macrophages or killer cells (see inset in Figure 12) to the site of infection. This lymphokine is known as macrophage migration inhibition factor (MIF);

iv) the production of 'activated' macrophages. This macrophage activating factor produces significant morphological changes in the macrophages which become metabolically very active and more effective in the destruction of ingested micro-organisms, such as mycobacteria.

It is important to realise that the course of a disease like TB depends on the effectiveness of the body's cell-mediated immune response. This is the final line of defence; normally impregnable; it can be severely weakened, as we have seen, by undue stress of one sort or another.

So I hope we can now begin to see the free-living animal as an open eco-system: a world in itself. A world in which the struggle to survive, between 'good' and 'evil', goes on just as we see it in our world, with invading micro-organisms the baddies, phagocytes the goodies, B-cells the undercover agents, and T-cells the mercenaries.

TB, so significant in human history and so central in the battle against infectious disease, must be confronted squarely. Dr Grange in 1982 stressed that

tuberculosis is still the most prevalent bacterial disease of man and is responsible (globally) for 5,000 deaths a day. TB is notoriously difficult to control and rapidly rears its ugly head wherever interest, awareness and attention are directed away from it. But it is rather surprising, in a climate of general apathy towards the worldwide tuberculosis situation, that the unfortunate badger is receiving so much hostile attention. Although there is no doubt that tuberculosis occurs in both cattle and badgers in the West Country, the evidence for its transmission from one to the other is purely circumstantial.

Infection begins when the organism responsible – the tubercle bacillus – is contracted by the host either through the lungs or intestines. It may be drunk with infected milk, hence the dangers of bovine TB before the days of pasteurisation and attested cattle; inhaled in droplets, this is aerosol infection caused by being in the close proximity of an infectious host; or inhaled with infected dust.

However, since the vast majority of people – certainly in industrialised countries – are infected in early childhood and yet have successfully overcome the challenge, one is naturally led to ask what it is that predisposes some to a progressive infection and not others? The answers are certainly to do with immunity and general health and vigour but that may not be the whole story. In adults, the commonest form of TB is of the respiratory kind; children are most susceptible to infection centred in the bones, glands and abdomen; worst of all, are tuberculosis meningitis, and miliary TB – a form of septicaemia which rampages through the body in a few weeks.

Sanitoria situated in mountains were traditional in the fight against TB. Fresh air was considered beneficial and before modern drugs such as streptomycin, it is possible that a change of air – a holiday in invigorating, pleasant and healthy environs – could be beneficial to those who could afford it. However, if this involved a stressful estrangement of a love bond, especially with children, the result, as we shall see, could be quite the opposite of the desired one. Sanitoria came to be reappraised; and of course the malign old fever hospitals where the poor went and where they received only rare visits from their relations because of fear of cross-infection, were deathtraps.

The skin test which most of us have at eleven years old indicates whether or not earlier exposure to the infection has induced a state of CMI (cell-mediated immunity). A reaction to tuberculin – a protein derived from bovine TB – showing as localised inflammation and occuring after one or two days indicates infection. This is known as 'delayed hypersensitivity', and the inflamed area, when examined histologically, will show infiltration by polymorphs (small phagocytes) and by large activated phagocytes – the killer cells. In humans,reactors will be treated. Uninfected tuberculin test negatives are usually vaccinated with BCG (bacillus of Calmette and Guerin). This contains live, attenuated bacilli which gives an individual a specific CMI response to *M. tuberculosis* but does not produce more than minor clinical symptoms of the disease. The immunity, acquired from BCG, means that the body can set up an immediate CMI response to any future invading tuberculosis pathogen.

It is important though to realise that in humans BCG does not actually prevent infection, it *limits* the multiplication and spread of the bacilli and the development of lesions. Thus, the vaccination reduces the number of cases where an individual becomes infectious.

In cattle, the tuberculin test (TT) (see Appendix I) works in the same way except that the delayed hypersensitivity response takes a day longer (i.e. 3 days), and reactors are slaughtered. They could be vaccinated but are not because the low level of infection so caused would invalidate future tests – that is to say it would become impossible to deduce whether that individual was reacting to the effect of the vaccination and was not dangerous, or was in a progressive infectious state. However, many critics belive that vaccination and the consequent creation of a resistant National Herd is the answer to TB in cattle, just as it is in humans, but current EEC regulations forbid it.

Unfortunately because tuberculin supresses rather than activates the badgers' T-cells, the test does not work with this species. In this the badger is no different to many other carnivores but it is a pity here because were a skin test possible MAFF would at least be able to identify infected badgers and either remove or vaccinate them. This would ameliorate the problem of bovine TB in badgers to such an extent that it would disappear: an enlightened, sophisticated and refined approach. Why MAFF are not devoting their mighty resources into finding a diagnostic live test for badgers and a range of other strategies is a subject to be discussed later on.

Early on in this chapter we discussed that consequential word 'eradicate', and maybe we should ask whether the eradication of TB is desirable or possible or both. The smallpox eradication scheme should not be cited as an exemplar for TB because there was considered to be no wildlife reservoir. It is the unknown prevalence of TB infection in various species of wildlife that makes its eradication impossible. Whether or not such an attempt is medically desirable depends on all sorts of factors – ethical and moral as well as scientific. Does, for instance, a base-level of incidence represent an insurance policy against future virulent and maybe spontaneous outbreaks emanating from unknown sources? If TB helps ameliorate overcrowding, appearing, for instance, where badgers are above the carrying capacity of their habitat, it is possible to see it not so much as a threat to individual badgers but as necessary to the species. There is certainly no justification in the ministry attempting to 'sell' TB as a threat to the future of the badger. And if one of TB's functions is to limit population size, curiously it suddenly appears as the farmers' friend, and the case for vaccination of cattle as the final safeguard becomes overwhelming. The disease then might be under control.

Before concluding this brief review of one of the world's most infamous diseases – once believed actually to consume people – I feel it is important to recognise the role of stress, and ask the question of veterinary medicine if it is not true that the human branch is not far advanced in at least one extremely important respect?

If so the reason is to be found in our speciesistic attitude to other lifeforms – broached at the very beginning. Do we not tend to deny other animals emotion? Indeed to mention emotion is often to invite cries of anthropomorphy or sentimentalism. It is left to the true visionary to light the way, though his beam is often ignored.

So it was that in 1688 Richard Morton wrote 'I have very often observed that a consumption of the lungs has had its origins in long and grievous passions of the mind'.

One hundred years later, an Austrian doctor, Leopold Auenbrugger – introducer of percussion as a means of discovering chest conditions, attributed consumption to 'affections of the mind'. Rene Laennec, inventor of the stethoscope, agreed. Another century, and Sir William Osler said 'it is just as important to know what is in a man's head as what is in his chest'. Sir William, a Canadian physician and medical historian, went against the current trend. He died in 1919, and between the wars these beliefs were dismissed as outmoded and unscientific.

However, psychosomatic medicine was beginning to display clinical signs itself. Flanders Dunbar observed that TB bacilli were everywhere. She asked 'why one person never gives the germs a chance, and another seems to provide a virtual broth of culture', and she showed a link between emotional crises and the broth in a number of cases. Still there was resistance.

Then in 1951, David Kissen began a series of investigations into the role played by emotional stress in the appearance of pulmonary TB. He had a tricky job in bringing emotions within the compass of scientific respectability. Patients coming to a local hospital with chest disorders were carefully questioned about their life stories: had they recently suffered a bereavement, a divorce, an unhappy love affair etc. There was of course a sector which was later found not to have TB, and thus a control group automatically presented itself.

The results spurred Kissen on to further investigations. One third (89) of the 267 patients in the sample were found to have TB, 65% of these had suffered from severe emotional distress, compared to only 26% of the 178 found not to be suffering from TB. Over 90% of those in the severe emotional-stress group had experienced a break in a strong love-bond. The next investigation dealt with those patients suffering relapses of the disease after a lengthy quiescence. Although the sample was smaller, the findings were even more startling: of the patients who had suffered a relapse, over 75% had preceding high emotional stress, compared to less than 12% of those who had not relapsed. Further investigations by Kissen and other workers showed that TB victims appeared to share 'an inordinate need for affection'. A careful questionnaire concerning family relationships, friendships and previous illnesses, and designed to be as objective as possible, revealed that once the control groups (constituted by those without TB) had been identified and separated, the outstanding personailty trait – shown by no less than 100% of the TB sufferers – was this inordinate need for affection. In the control group, the figure plummetted to 16%.

Suddenly a new way of looking at TB cycles emerges. The rise of TB during wartime used to be attributed to deprivation but if this was so why was there not an equivalent or even greater rise during the great depression of the early 1930's?

Kissen pointed out that while there had been physical privations, emotional security was not particularly threatened. In wartime, however, 'the threat to personal or family relationships was as great as could be', and there were numerous cruelly broken love-bonds. The situation in Jersey during World War II is interesting: TB soared during the time of the foreign invasion and dropped again immediately after the Occupation. The islanders did not suffer unduly from malnutrition or physical hardship.

Rene and Jean Dubose in their work *The White Plague* noted that TB flared in Red Indian reservations 'after they had lost the freedom of their favourite hunting grounds'. To a Red Indian this would represent a broken love-bond of the greatest magnitude.

Kissen's inspirational work seemed to come too late. By 1958, when he published his *Emotional Factors in Pulmonary Tuberculosis*, the incidence of human TB was falling thanks to modern drugs, improved living conditions and a general lack of strife. Yet, as Brian Inglis says in his review of *The Diseases of Civilisation*, Kissen's findings are valuable in coming to a better understanding of the mechanics of infection. They demonstrate, he claims, the need to take into account risk factors other than the infecting agent.

The threat to humans from the bovine strain, which used to claim so many victims, was virtually eliminated by the test-and-slaughter of infected cattle. The residue left in wildlife and the environment generally cannot be tackled in the same way. Try as they do, officialdom cannot manage a wild population as though it were a domestic or human one. They keep trying, and are dismissive about the role of stress. Once it was acknowledged, but because of inherent difficulties in quantifying it – as in the inter-war period – such factors are now disliked by the mathematical and statistical biologists currently in vogue.

Have we in the past, and are we now, grossly underestimating the capacity of social animals to feel emotion? If so, what are the consequences for a social group of badgers – in other words, a tightly-knit extended family – of an insensitive and heavy-handed culling operation? And what if the slaughter is protracted and inefficient? It seems not unreasonable to expect increased incidence, relapses and a general lowering of natural resistance. Moreover, the indirect disruption caused to neighbouring groups and their inter-relationships, deeply ingrained – often over many centuries – can perhaps be imagined. The boundaries between badger tribes represent an equilibrium – where countering force and influence is spent – and where an uneasy alliance could represent security. A system of scent signals, like banner waving, normally forestalls physical conflict.

When normality is destroyed, by nature or man, anxiety increases, and health and rational behaviour take a dive – in man as in nature.

THREE

The Law and the Omen

Though scarcely half as big, dimute and small

(Clare)

It should have surprised no-one when the cumbersome wheels of law moved to protect the badger. A truly civilised society would have moved long before. Lord Arran's Badgers Act 1973 seemed merely to be reflecting public opinion: badger-digging was anachronistic – a relic from centuries before – something on its way to merciful oblivion following the fiendish baiting contests – which most people believed were already as remote as bear-baiting and cock-fighting. The Act was seen as the final act in the tragedy of the British badger. The pathetic human remnants who still satisfied their sadism in the spectacle of a single shy wild animal being torn to living pieces by a pack of perverted dogs, were surely on their way into the chamber of horrors along with Spanish Inquisitors and the Marquis de Sade. They would remain as a nightmare.

Sadly, reality was less creditable. Any student of life knows that fate always holds the best hand. And at one throw, usually backed up by several more in quick succession, can poleaxe any strategy built on logic and reason.

One of the prime movers in the fight to protect the badger was E Jane Ratcliffe, and in her book *Through the Badger Gate* she recounts graphically the enervating tedium of piloting a Bill through parliament, especially with an apathetic Home Office continually turning down appeals with stereotyped letters, as they had for twenty years. Then:

By coincidence, in February 1973, two badger protection Private Members Bills were put forward at the same time, one a comprehensive total protection bill by Lord Arran in the House of Lords and the other a very limited anti-digging bill by Mr Peter Hardy in the House of Commons.

Many amendments were proposed to Lord Arran's Bill, and because of the difficulties involved in getting all-out protection, carefully worded amendments had to be devised. Even the attitude of the Home

Office changed to almost friendly. 'Each stage succeeded the former as Lord Arran skilfully piloted his Bill through the Lords until its final approval on May 1st 1973 when it was passed in the House of Commons'.

As it was late in the 1973 session, Peter Hardy magnanimously dropped his Bill and saw Lord Arran's amended Bill through its many procedures. 'Shortly after, the Queen gave her Royal Assent, so there appeared on the Statute Book at last a Badger Act [*designed*] to make the life of the much maligned and persecuted badger so much safer'.

Under the Act it was intended to be an offence for any person to kill or to attempt to kill, injure, take, cruelly ill-treat, dig for or use badger-tongs on any badger. Also, to sell, offer for sale or have in his possession any live badger...though the fines were low at £100 even by 1973 standards.

Improved protection came in the Wild Life and Countryside Act 1981. But still it was insufficient to prevent the scheming of the pathologically cruel. They came to see that in the fox lay their absolution.

Until Dr David Clark's Amendment Bill in 1985, there was little hope either for the badger being dug out or the fox waiting as an alibi in a sack – 'proof', should the spade brigade need it, that badgers were the last thing on their mind. Dr Clark's sensitive amendment soon fell foul of the fox-hunters afraid that it might impinge on their peculiar pleasure. And the fox and badger, enemies in fable, still got in each other's way. Only a massive and unparalleled MPs' mailbag prevented a terrible corruption of justice.

But we must return to the early 1970s. 1970, itself, was European Conservation Year, and saw the beginning of Jane Ratcliffe's lobbying to protect the badger legally. Progress was slow, and the general public only casually sympathetic.

Elsewhere in Britain there was another problem. The Ministry of Agriculture's campaign to eradicate tuberculosis from cattle had not been as effective in parts of the West Country, notably in West Penwith – the westernmost tip of England near Penzance – as it had been elsewhere. It was not known why, though badgers had apparently been suspected by some farmers for as long as twenty years. A ministry enquiry by a team of four veterinarians – the Richards' Report published in 1972 – suggested a broad response, though events in Gloucestershire were soon to overtake and obliterate such logical progress. MAFF's Chief Veterinary Officer in his Foreword wrote:

It is clear from the findings that no one factor can be said to be responsible for the present situation but that a combination of factors together contribute to the perpetuation and spread of bovine tuberculosis in the area.

The authors wrote:

Tuberculosis in cattle is usually contracted from other infected cattle and the environment which they have contaminated... Cattle may be infective at any stage during the course of the disease.

They also stated that in their view

the intensification of livestock production in an area where there is a relatively high incidence of bovine tuberculosis militates against its successful eradication.

It is clear MAFF then attached a lot of importance to agricultural practices. The poor standard of fencing seen in West Penwith was considered 'a major factor in the perpetuation and spread of tuberculosis' in that it enabled contact between cows on neighbouring farms. Late in 1985, evidence from the State veterinary service in N. Ireland confirmed this. The practice of spreading slurry or manure on pasture, and then allowing grazing immediately afterwards was partly responsible. MAFF stated that 'the dissemination of tuberculosis in this area, both within the herd and from infected to neighbouring herds, is largely related to husbandry and management practices'.

Pigs were considered a possible source of trouble since they were susceptible to the disease but not tested. It was felt, in a nice turn of understatement, 'that it would be helpful to establish whether pigs in this area are infected'. Goats were considered not to be implicated, but dogs and cats, which *are* susceptible, and 'which are commonly found' were not indicated because of a lack of evidence, which is hardly surprising since it wasn't looked for – nor is it still.

Turning to wildlife, we notice the first signs of official concern about badgers. 'The recent isolation of bovine tubercle bacilli from badgers and badger faeces in Gloucestershire...underlines the need to determine the part played by wildlife.'

The Gloucestershire case (Badger #1) was what some had been waiting for. In April 1971, a badger, infected with bovine TB, was found on a troubled farm in the south of the county. The farmer in question, as luck would have it, was also a MAFF vet, and though eight years later he is reported to have admitted that the evidence incriminating the badger was still 'totally circumstantial' it was at the time clutched at as *proof* wherever there was an inexplicable breakdown.

Dr Paul Barrow reviewed the evidence in 1982, and pointed out that by the end of 1971, eight of eleven carcasses, and three of five faecal specimens showed the disease. 'The die,' he says 'had been definitely cast'. We should not have been surprised, for elsewhere in the world there were known reservoirs of infection in wildlife: in Switzerland with the badger way back in the 1950's, and in New Zealand with the possum. Tuberculous roe deer were also found at that time; and due to the badger's penchant for scavenging they were thought likely to have then become infected. In an American piece of work published in 1971, W R Snider *et al* found a high incidence rate in cats and dogs, and felt that they might be involved to a greater extent than was generally believed up to that time in the USA. Yet, incidentally, by the end of 1984, only 22 cats and *no* dogs had been officially investigated in southwest England (this is discussed more fully in Chapter 10).

Large scale badger sampling began in 1972. By 1974, 142 of 1,200 showed evidence of the disease; some badgers clearly had it, but whether or not they actually became infectious and *spread* the disease was quite another matter.

In an attempt to prove just that, some small scale experiments were carried out at MAFF's Central Veterinary Labratory (CVL), Weybridge (see Chapter 10). Otherwise, the evidence rested on what Lord Zuckerman called 'Argument by Exclusion', 'Association', 'The Chain of Evidence', 'Population Density' and 'Regional Incidence' – in other words – circumstantial (this will be examined in Chapter 6).

Ironic, though, that at the time Lord Arran's Bill was gaining its Royal Assent, fate was stacking its hand against the badger. Concurrently with the implementation of the protective legislation in February 1974, MAFF were killing more and more badgers in an attempt to prove their case. The National Farmers' Union (NFU) were not unreasonably clamouring for action as they had been led to believe that the badger's guilt was *fait accompli*. Some farmers had lost a great deal of money despite compensation, a few had even gone out of business. One farm in Dorset was paid £79,000 over a series of outbreaks. MAFF naturally wished to reduce this level of compensation, and they also needed to reassure farmers that something on the ground was being done; this, it was claimed, was also necessary to help minimise the illegal slaughter of badgers by ignorant farmers.

The ministry, confident they could control badgers, were no doubt grateful their target had turned out not to be a small rodent, insectivore, invertebrate or bird, but one of large size, living in recognised and settled places, giving clear signs of its habits. The badger had appeared on cue. Many observers feel that from this point on, MAFF, believing the problem solved, classically ceased to question it.

Doubt about the extent of the problem set in later but so much confidence abounded in the early days, that MAFF even set up a demonstration of the available methods for farmers who could be encouraged to kill the badgers themselves. As a matter of fact, *Cymag* – a cyanide preparation – increasingly used since World War II against rabbits and foxes was also often used on farms and estates to kill badgers despite this having been made illegal in the Protection of Animals Act of 1911 and 1912, and the Agriculture Act 1947. Since foxes often occupy badgers' sets, the phoney plea went out – as with badger digging until 1985 – that foxes were the actual target.

The somewhat audacious demonstration backfired. A lactating mother was found ensnared with a lacerated udder. The RSPCA protested and a private court action was brought against one of the ministry pest officers and the Minister of Agriculture (Fred Peart) himself, on the grounds of having transgressed the Badgers Act. Conviction was avoided on a technicality but the repercussions have still not subsided.

MAFF thought again, this time consulting others. Snares were now ruled out, so was cage-trapping – considered to be too time-consuming and cumbersome. Gassing began to emerge as the preferred option.

The Badgers Act appeared to have discouraged some of the illegal persecution – casual diggers being deterred by the prospect of litigation if not the derisory fines. The pathological, of course, are deterred by nothing but when the tap of official gas was turned on, and badgers began to die in vast numbers, it was obviously asking too much of the earthy vandal. Why should he lay off what he had always regarded as legitimate quarry just when the same forces of law, which were deterring him, were embarking on their own policy of wholesale slaughter? Either something was prohibited, for reasons he could or could not understand, or it wasn't.

So, not only did MAFF systematically begin to exterminate badgers from entire areas, they did it by using gas, which had been outlawed in the Protection of Animals Act 1911 and 1912. It was the Badgers Act itself which enabled licenses to be granted: 'for the purpose of preventing the spread of disease to kill or take badgers within an area specified in the licence by any means so specified'. An obscure clause in the Wild Creatures and Wild Plants Act 1975 enabled gas to be specified in such licences.

The law now seemed an ass to some country people: one government department was busy eradicating badgers while another was endevouring to protect them. Their credulity must have been stretched yet further by the Wildlife and Countryside Act 1981. This abolished the category of 'authorised persons' which had since 1973 allowed anonymous and privileged landowners to do virtually anything to badgers, providing 'wilful cruelty' could not be proved, and increased the maximum fine to a more realistic £1,000.

By the time this bastardised Act was born in a weak, deformed and mutilated state, MAFF had killed at least 10,000 badgers. Most of these, moreover, had been killed not with cruelty which could be attributed to wilfulness but to ignorance (this is discussed more fully in Chapter 5).

FOUR

The Case Against Brock

Go out and track the badger to his den

(Clare)

As we approach the twenty-first century, and our lives become inextricably ensnared in the fastidious world of the microchip, I keep hoping that somewhere in the slipstream of technology the brutal and insensitive will be caught up and whisked along a pace or two. Why the reverse seems to apply we will consider later, but I hope at least we need not waste space here by looking for crimes in the badger that warrant the more extreme forms of punishment handed out to it.

The upsurge of unprovoked violence is discussed later, here the question is: why, if the badger is a blameless inhabitant of the rural scene, are powerful hands raised against it? What are the factors that set some farmers, landowners, veterinarians and agriculture ministry officals against it?

A few land managers, it is true, distrust to the point of hysteria anything which moves or grows unless it enjoys their sanction. They tend to grant this only to resources which can be seen as profitable. These farmers are businessmen; they promote farming as though it were an industry concerned only with yields, profits and cash-flow, and nothing very much to do with nature. This kind of land user cannot concentrate on any rationale that leads away from the main commercial preoccupation; if it threatens to do so, it is regarded as hostile.

I don't know how many come into this category, no one does, but one keeps hearing about them – usually from genuine farmers – and I'm sure the damage they do both to the land and their trade is out of all proportion to their number. Some farmers are certainly ardent conservationists, many just try to earn a reasonable living in as decent a way as possible; but there are some whose attitudes are cruel and unaccommodating. They might have a lot of land or a few acres, but they are characterized by a blind arrogance, and it is up to their fellows to control them if they truly wish theirs to be regarded as an honourable profession. The stewardship of the earth affects everyone, and can no longer be left prey to the whim of those who might destroy it through ignorance.

The badger is central to this in Britain. We have already regarded it as the most significant wild animal left in our countryside. Though it is declining steadily, it is not yet an endangered species. (How curious is felt the trepidation, confronted daily by the abyss of eternal extinction, when daring to speak of an organism which has not yet reached that precipice – as though it is somehow demeaned.)

It is the badger's very significance that creates most of its problems. Were it smaller, living aloft in trees, it would bother and be bothered less. Through just a touching 'innocence' it can make rather a lot of itself. Like a small child, who, to the annoyance of a houseproud or busy mother, will untidy a room simply by being there, the badger will untidy the edge of a field or a hedge. It will excavate its tunnels and chambers with dogged persistence, not realising or caring that the spoil it trundles out has to go somewhere. Neither did its evolution take into account the development of heavy machinery, with the result that the badger's burrows are sometimes at insufficient depth to prevent tractor wheels from crashing through the roof. Once a forest dweller, he had little choice but to excavate around the secure and tangled roots of trees. Badgers can also seriously undermine walls and earth banks, and occasionally small buildings; very often, though, the damage looks more severe than is actually the case.

Some non-conformist, inexperienced or particularly stubborn badgers will endeavour to live in the middle of open fields, and thereby cause all sorts of problems to perplexed farmers. They do this either because there had once been a spinney or hedge there, and are reluctant to give up a traditional residence, or simply because there is nowhere else to go. Badgers live in highly structured territories; during times of rising population usually after a succession of green, damp summers and mild winters with little or no human persecution, and after a territory has reached its carrying capacity, subordinate badgers may be pushed out into unsuitable habitat.

Sick badgers occasionally come into barns, byres or some other kind of outbuilding – near a source of food – and either recuperate quietly or die. On a friend's farm one August, an old albino badger took up residence in a sheep creep in an open field for ten days before disappearing. On the same farm, another appeared not to move for three weeks from the corner of a large barn. And it is established that badgers which have sustained serious injury will remain in a coma for many days in a process of self-healing.

Other misdemeanours are classed as trespass, though that is even harder to justify with a wild animal than it is with a wandering human.

Usually such nuisance results when new barriers are erected across badger's traditional scent-trails. He will scrape his way under, push through or clamber over as he would past a natural obstacle like a fallen tree. Fortunately this minor problem is decreasing as 'badger-gates', which allow Brock through but keep rabbits out become better known.

If ever a wild animal could be said to live its life in a rut, it must be the badger. An undisturbed run can become exactly that as generations of badgers plod to and fro along it. Sadly, again, their design and evolution, while equipping them to shrug off fallen trees and boulders, did nothing to prepare them for the more serious obstacles of man. His barriers of hedges and walls are nothing compared to the roads and railways they are supposed to delimit.

These strips of concrete, steel and tarmac laid by man like a cat's cradle all over the land, facilitating his insatiable appetite for always being somewhere else, might appear to a badger, especially during construction, as an interesting novelty – giving different foraging possibilities and unimpeded passage. When completed and open to traffic, the badgers will continue to use the same general route to their feeding grounds and neighbouring sets, maybe even approving in passing of the clear firm footing. The massacre which follows is largely accidental. Drivers could certainly propel their lethal vehicles more considerately but by and large they don't *blame* the badger when they hit one, even if it causes some superficial damage – which is quite possible with an animal weighing 30lbs. However, most drivers, even those downright hostile to animals' rights, endeavour to avoid running one over, and involuntary swerving can cause serious accidents. For this reason, at least, planning authorities and architects are generally sympathetic if asked to incorporate into a new road a safe passage for wildlife. The cost, compared to the total, is infinitesimal: one every few miles equals one hundreth of one per cent of the total expenditure.

When a badger reaches the pasture on which it likes to roam it can again, just by being there, upset a tetchy owner who ignores or fails to see the good in the beast. Its diet which, on paper consists mostly of earthworms, insects, and a range of other miscellaneous invertebrates, carrion, fruit, roots and vegetables, includes great quantities of animals not generally regarded as agricultural allies – cockchafer grubs, leatherjackets, slugs, snails, nests of rats, moles, voles, mice, rabbits and wasps. In spring and early summer, especially before they were decimated by myxomatosis, rabbits formed a major part of the badger's diet.

Any bulky animal ranging over a farm will inevitably from time to time cross the farmer's path. Sometimes he does commit the metaphor but mostly the transgression is merely physical. The most serious crime he is accused of concerns the killing of healthy lambs and poultry. The evidence for the former is so tenuous that if it occurs at all it is so rare as to be freakish. The vast majority of allegations are found, on cross-examination, to be based on myth and association.

The badger is a scavenger, an insectivore and an omnivore – above all he is an opportunist. To take at face value his classification in the Order Carnivora is to be led astray by the taxonomists. The badger is not a grand hunter: he is a forager, a rooter and a gleaner. A glance at his shape tells us this, also that he must be a very good one if able to sustain his substance on one of earthworms. Such a laboriously acquired diet needs to be extended whenever and wherever possible. He will forage where the reward is worth the expenditure of time and energy, and will certainly take advantage of farming by-products – adapting his perambulations to agricultural cycles.

At lambing time, badgers will avail themselves of waste products including afterbirth, and stillborn and sickly lambs. If those who would accuse him of more could analyse their prejudice, they would see that in classic scavenging tradition, the badger is quickly on the scene, actively contributing harmful waste to the recycle of growth.

A local NFU official proudly claimed at a meeting to have actually seen a badger attacking and biting the tails off his lambs. He exacted his retribution by illegally killing two. When pressed on the evidence, he declared 'I'd know a badger footprint anywhere': Brock, the forager, is doomed; another fable born. Other 'eye-witness' accounts degenerate similarly into amateurish detective work – often the result, it seems, of wishful thinking. We all seek to blame others, and divert attention from ourselves; it just so happens that in the countryside the most convenient and silent scapegoat is usually a wild animal. Neglect of this gambit can result in damaged pride.

Much the same goes when rearing pheasants. Gamekeepers have traditionally killed badgers on the grounds that they are large, have teeth and move. The archetypal gamekeeper is a very simple creature with poor vision. He is generally unable to see shades of grey, and reacts only to black and white; all experiences are thus quickly and easily assessed. An animal is good or bad: if it cannot be seen to represent direct profit, it must be either a nuisance or a threat. Fortunately the archetype slowly evolves. Badgers are less harrassed by gamekeepers today than they have ever been but some still see them as a threat to pheasant eggs, poults and even the sitting hens themselves. Stomach and faecal analyses and observation just do not bear out this quite understandable belief. A badger's preferred diet takes it away from cover at this critical time and out into pasture. There are cases on record of entire clutches of gamebirds being hatched and reared successfully near badger sets – some nests being amongst the very entrance holes themselves with the badgers passing disinterestedly by only inches away.

There is a surprising twist though when we come to hear the case of the raided poultry run. This crime blackens the fox's image more than anything; such attacks, so close to our own homes, are seen as audacious, cunning and insolent. And yet many could be so easily avoided with no tragic losses or blood-letting.

Just as it is the householder's responsibility to keep the domestic animals of others out of his garden, so it is the husbandman's responsibility to keep his stock secure. When poultry in particular are lost we must ask fairly and squarely if we had done all we could to prevent it. An honest answer would often be 'no'.

The fox manages to highlight in a particularly graphic way the chinks in our armour but it is actually easier to guard against fox attack than that of rogue badger. A determined badger takes a lot of stopping and will not be deterred, as will a fox, merely by secure wire-netting. A badger with a taste for poultry is rare but a real problem, and can be shot under licence. Such a rogue is usually old, sick or finds it impossible for some other reason – often climatic, such as a drought in mid-summer – to find sufficient natural food.

Prolonged dry weather is the badger's worst natural enemy. In high summer, the staple earthworm burrows deep to aestivate and conserve moisture, and the autumn harvest is not yet ripe for collection. The badger returns to other resources, exceptionally this can be poultry but more normally it becomes a gleaner of wheat. If particularly hard-pressed it will resort to the unripe standing corn, and forages extensively over stubble. It is not really adapted for such foods, and its digestive juices are unable to break down the fibrous material. This period of hardship can mean that cubs born earlier, in the spring, will be hard pushed to build up the reserves needed to get them through their first winter, which is the severest test of all for resident wild animals and birds.

'Straw-rolling' can also gain a few enemies at this time of the year, but it is rare to find a farmer who holds this crime, uncompounded, strongly against the badger.

Of course all these relatively minor transgressions – real or imagined – do go, in some parts of the country, to compound what is seen as by far the badger's most major crime. This is revealed by the fear – real or imagined – that he is largely to blame for spreading bovine tuberculosis to cattle. Accepting for the time being that TB in cattle is still a problem of sufficient moment to warrant an exhaustive eradication campaign, and that there is no alternative method of control (see Chapters 10 & 11), we must assess the badger's guilt as a vector.

Unfortunately the experts can't agree; that's a bad sign and a bad start.

It is an emotional subject this, even to most of those who fiercely deny being prone to such weaknesses. We must not deny emotion, for it reveals much about the human psyche, and lies inextricably bound up with humanity. It colours every decision we make. Maybe it is possible to be trained in cold and utter logic but such strictures should not be the main part of any biological curriculum. Objectivity is quite a different matter but the choice of object is itself highly coloured; and I doubt if the means by which we strike at our object is altogether of neutral hue.

As a crude example: a line of research into invertebrate physiology can quite reasonably, it would seem, claim many lives but a parallel enquiry into vertebrates would be much more rigorously scrutinised, if permitted at all. That is a value judgement. More closely akin: one might assess the relative subjectivity of rats and harvest mice similarly.

So, since we admit an emotional factor in this equation, there is an onus to try to assess its correct value. It is a factor which must not be overvalued and yet cannot be overlooked.

Despite the knowledge that the link has never been satisfactorily demonstrated under reasonable controlled conditions and certainly not naturally, the badger probably is, in some circumstances, a disease risk to cattle but there are perplexing anomalies for those who seek absolutes: infection in badgers associating with healthy cattle, and herd breakdowns where, try as one might, the source cannot be traced to badgers – that is to say, no infected badgers could be found (this does not mean they do not exist).

This fundamental link is of crucial importance, and has been from the start of badger investigation back in the early seventies. Critics of MAFF find it extraordinary that work into the exact mode of transmission has been neglected. In its place there has been assumption and deduction. When embarking on a massive, costly and highly contentious programme of eradication, there is a demand for fundamentals.

Here we are concerned only with badger-to-cow cross-infection though the badger is only one of eighteen possible sources (see Appendix II). It is to be hoped that he does not become the easy option – a tool of appeasement. The bacilli can be spread by several routes: via faeces, urine, sputum, pus from lungs or bite wounds; and it might be present in carcasses and old bedding. A cow might also conceivably inhale the bacilli during an encounter with an infectious badger, but the likely routes are all *indirect*. No-one has yet accused tuberculous badgers of dashing round savaging cows. One would expect cross-infection to occur via pasture contaminated with products or by aerosols of exhaled bacilli.

We can begin to see the fog creeping in; a fog which denies direct exit. The Wildlife Link Badger Working Group, which includes some of the country's leading experts, states

that some environmental contamination (from badgers) is inevitable... If the MAFF preliminary procedure...gives no indication of the origin of infection and if tuberculous badgers are in 'close proximity' to a breakdown, MAFF assumes that there is sufficient evidence to attribute the breakdown to badgers... Thus wild animals such as badgers are found 'guilty by association'...

One way to avoid placing undue reliance on such highly circumstantial evidence would be to develop to a viable stage the sophisticated amino acid typing technique devised by Grange in 1976, and used by Barrow to identify so far at least 31 strains of the bovine tubercle bacillus. The precise strain of bacillus involved in a herd breakdown could then be identified; any identical strain found in a local badger community would then be the *likely* culprit, and the case for removing those badgers would be much stronger. If, however, the strain is found to be different, the badger would be proven 'innocent'.

'Guilt' in the badger assumes transmission of the bacilli in one direction: from badger to cow. In Cornwall 1984, MAFF were visiting farms to check out the badgers eighteen months after the initial herd breakdown thus making it impossible to gauge accurately the prevalence of disease in badgers *before* the breakdown. Swift pathological examination could clarify this, but MAFF attach little importance to understanding sources of infection in badgers. Such deliberations are considered irrelevant and academic, and yet the lack of this knowledge – academic maybe to MAFF's stated task in any particular case – makes long-term control of the disease very much more difficult. So, while it is not directly applicable to this chapter, it is obviously dangerous to attribute an outbreak *to* badgers if they had been victims of a tuberculous cow, another local reservoir or some itinerant vector. However, this attribution is common, and is one of the reasons accounting for the badger's portrayal as a scapegoat. If MAFF are to avoid this charge, they must demonstrate clearly the badger's involvement in each and every outbreak of TB in cattle before they begin to disrupt social groups in a way which might open up neighbouring farms to an increased risk.

Not only are MAFF disinterested in the origins of infection in badgers, they also underestimate the prevalence of infection in cattle, according to Dr David Macdonald, one of Britain's most brilliant zoologists and a leading authority on the subject, placing far too much reliance on the accuracy of the intradermal tuberculin test. They seem 'surprisingly optimistic' in assuming that all save a few of the 600-900 cattle – even accounting for the 'false-positives' (see below) – reacting positively to the skin test do so before they become infectious. Beef cattle are tested less frequently (only every 2-3 years in most regions) than dairy herds (yearly in the problem areas), and since a TB lesion can develop in a few months, there is ample time for an infected animal to spread the disease. Animals with small closed lesions can pass the test repeatedly before a new stress or – for example, being put on the market, movement, poor management or some other disease/treatment – lowers their natural resistance, causing a lesion to burst open and become infectious. High yielding dairy cows are already highly stressed. Albeit rarely, animals at an advanced stage of the disease do not react to the test, and may spread the disease for significant periods before finally succumbing themselves. The Richards' report in 1972 recorded 20 cattle classified as negative in a test but which were tuberculous.

The test is inaccurate the other way too, and very many cows react falsely to the test. These so-called 'false-positives' account for nearly *half* all reactors. Work published in 1975 showed that of 88 reactors only 58 (66%) were positive for the bovine tubercle bacillus: all had tissues cultured and were examined for lesions. MAFF data since 1975 show that about half of all reactors have visible lesions (VL). When asked in 1984 what proportion of the remainder – the cattle with no visible lesions (NVL) – had bovine TB, the reply was surprising, and stated that despite virtually all NVL reactors having undergone microscopic culture of their tissues, bovine tubercle bacilli were recovered from only 4.2%.

In 1975 moreover, the tuberculin test was refined: a purified protein derivative (PPD) from *M. bovis* replacing the old *M. tuberculosis* PPD. This increased the specificity of the test, and yet, as the number of true-positives fell, the false positives became numerically more significant. False-positives are probably due to sensitization to mycobacteria other than from the bovine strain. These include *M. avium* – despite the comparative skin test (see Appendix I), *M. phlei, M. fortuitum* and the non-culturable types that produce skin lesions.

This indicates that almost *half* all reactors are *not* infected with bovine TB. And though this seems to halve the problem, improved techniques for identifying microscopic but open lesions, developed in N. Ireland, are showing that a surprisingly high proportion of cattle are infectious, though the pattern of TB in N. Ireland is different to mainland UK, with fewer badgers than in the south-west of England and larger cattle breakdowns.

It is unfortunate that any farmer with a reactor will not unreasonably now immediately suspect the badger, and demand action from the ministry which is taken as support for their policy. If action should not be forthcoming, for whatever reason, he may take action himself – so hard has the case against the badger been pushed. Some of the critical evidence is discussed in Chapter 10.

But there *is* a case to be made, and to a large extent it relies on the theory that the disease exists in 'pockets', and can, therefore, by direct 'fire-brigade' action, be contained and wiped out. Of course pockets are of no fixed size and can expand or contract to represent the prevailing situation. In Cornwall, as I write, an operation extending north from the south coast has met up with one moving south from the north, while elsewhere, in contrast, a pocket consists of a single breakdown.

However, there is certainly a south-west 'pocket', within which the disease in cattle is largely concentrated around certain distinct foci – the 'problem areas'. Within these, the incidence in badgers also appears to be higher, but whether that is cause or effect has not yet been satisfactorily shown.

It seems certain that the role of the badger will remain unknown until a typing system is perfected and the epidemiology of the disease itself is more fully understood. Until such time, badgers will often be convicted by association, and slaughtered on a hit-and-miss, hope-for-the-best basis – this may be an official 'fire-brigade' action or an independent farmer's own illegal vendetta. Either way, it is a result of subjective assessment.

In modern land use, farming and business practices are sacrosanct while wildlife is expendable.

FIVE

'Dealing With The Problem'

And put a sack within the hole, and lye...

(Clare)

In a fresh look at the evidence concerning 'the role of badgers in tuberculosis infections of cattle' published in *New Scientist* in October 1984, David Macdonald looked back at the problem.

After outlining the success of the pre-badger Attested Herd Scheme ('a triumph of veterinary medicine'), Macdonald remembers the 1971 Gloucestershire case which focussed attention on the badger. By April 1973, out of 165 badger carcasses examined in the south-west, 36 (21.8%) had been found diseased. By the end of 1973, considerable data had been collected, and of 1200 badger samples, 142 (11.8%) showed evidence of the bacilli. Macdonald writes:

In 1975, concluding that a reservoir of infection among badgers in the south-west explained the persistence there of TB in cattle, MAFF began to eradicate badgers. Hydrogen cyanide gas was pumped into all the setts found within a one-kilometre radius of infected herds where badgers were implicated. This time-honoured, albeit often ineffective approach to wildlife management led to the gassing of more than 4000 setts between August 1975 and June 1982, with little demonstrable effect other than to inflame public wrath and scientific debate to a level never previously achieved by any wildlife issue in Britain. Today, nine years on, the persistence of bovine tuberculosis in the 'problem areas' of the south-west is still as stubborn as it was in 1975, and its epidemiology is hardly more explicable now than then.

The gassing regime was interrupted by Lord Zuckerman's enquiry; for about a year – from September 1979 – it was suspended except to maintain freedom of badgers in areas already cleared. The run-up to gassing was briefly described in Chapter 4; snares were ruled out after the bungled demonstration even though it is a method preferred by some experienced fieldworkers who maintain that if properly set and maintained, and inspected every one or two hours, they can be more humane for badgers than cage-traps. They are also, of course, far less cumbersome to transport around, much cheaper and less prone to interference and dilapidation. On the other hand, snares call for more skilled use and frequent inspection throughout the night by staff on overtime and in need of on-site mobile accommodation.

Snares are disliked by most people because they are unselective and can catch non-target species such as foxes, deer, cats and dogs which are likely to be strangled. Because of a badger's wedge shape, snares set specifically for them have a large loop so that the victim can walk right into it before getting caught around the stomach.

I believe the unlicensed use of all snares is evil and immoral. The self-locking type is now mercifully illegal although manufacturers soon applied their devious minds to circumventing this act of compassion.

The use of cage-traps is outlined in Chapter 7, but their main advantage over snares is that once set and baited they have to be inspected only once every 24 hours, albeit soon after dawn, and each hit-squad is able to cover a much larger area. However, gassing, after consultation with interested parties including animal welfare groups – most of whom reluctantly accepted the need to control badgers in some areas, was chosen. MAFF, probably unwittingly, had set up its stall well, and most farmers and many other people too were coming automatically to suspect the badger.

MAFF truly did believe it had found the final obstacle along its somewhat Utopian and primrose-studded path to total eradication. Others were less sure and asked questions that MAFF were unable to answer convincingly. Unfortunately, these questions instead of ringing warning bells and spurring MAFF to a holistic approach, had the opposite effect: they closed ranks, dug themselves in and erected a stockade around their case. They tried, in short, to indicate that the badger, and the badger alone, was guilty. In doing so they recommitted the classic error of the poor sleuth, and the evidence was bent to fit the theory.

As we shall see later, the truth must be at risk when a scientist works for a politician. This calls for a very special kind of scientist, and there are some, but in general the system works against integrity and favours obsequiousness. Phil Drabble, the well-known broadcaster on country matters, has no time for bureaucrats (few naturalists can have), and has accused the ministry of incompetence many times. His direct style may not please all conservationists but by voicing fundamental fears he aims at the heart. I feel that any incompetence is a sign of the problem rather than the problem itself; it is the inevitable blemish which results from cosmetic evidence – of trying to make a different picture to the one on the lid of the puzzle. I have to tell my young children, when they get frustrated with their puzzle, to look at the picture. Phil Drabble is telling the ministry to find the picture.

In a much earlier *New Scientist* article, published in November 1977,

David Coffey, an eminent veterinary surgeon once employed by MAFF, wrote:

So long as the veterinary profession acts strictly in accordance with scientific method it will continue to enjoy the respect of the scientific community and the general public. When those principles are sacrificed for the short-term and often dubious benefits of political expediency, however, it is not beyond the bounds of possibility that it will make an ass of itself.

I suspect that the state veterinary service is currently so engaged. In what can only be described as a sordid attempt to gain transient respite from the pressures imposed by its political masters and the scorn of the farming community, the state veterinary service has succumbed to the easy option of a scapegoat to explain the embarrassing persistence of bovine tuberculosis in the west country. Badgers have been selected for government gas.

Coffey goes on to examine the early evidence for and against gassing, and finishes by saying:

The discovery of bovine tuberculosis in a traumatised badger may in retrospect prove fortuitous. What is surely certain is the absence of adequate scientific evidence to support the current policy. To permit its continuation may prove a travesty of state veterinary medicine.

The meat of this sandwich is part broth – a statistical broth 'which would poison any self-respecting statistician at the first sip'. Coffey also says that the stockade erected 'to protect the policy of badger slaughter would embarrass an innumerate recruit to a kindergarten'.

Coffey, in 1977, was surely right to question the early evidence just as I must re-examine it, for it is what the entire badger campaign is founded on. MAFF claimed that the disease was more common in badgers than all other fauna; perhaps they were right – perhaps they still are – but on what was this plank, central to their argument, placed?

It was based on results of 4,468 badger samples compared to 1,344 from 24 other species: an average of 56 per species, 11 of which were sampled by fewer than ten individuals, and a further 11 by less than 100. To bring this into perspective, Dr Paul Barrow, an expert bacteriologist, has made it graphically clear how misleading it can be to rely on unmethodical small chance samples: 'The extent of infection- ...can be estimated only by large scale sampling over large areas', and, in passing, reminds MAFF again that they would be wrong to place undue importance on the results on some of his own earlier work with John Gallagher of MAFF (see Chapter 10), stating that results obtained from one exercise cannot necessarily be extrapolated to other situations.

Barrow, in a 1983 note, shows that to be near certain of discovering a 5% character (in this case $M. bovis$) nearly one hundred random samples are needed more or less simultaneously. If the character sought occurs at a prevalence less than this – as could well be the case – obviously a very much larger sample would be needed. To be 95% sure

Fig 5 Binomial extension giving guidelines of optimum sample sizes when looking for a character such as TB. Of all wild animals only the badger has been sampled in large numbers. (*Prepared by Dr Paul Barrow and reproduced by courtesy of New Scientist*)

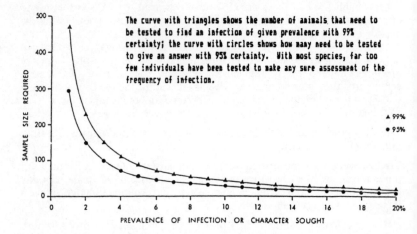

The curve with triangles shows the number of animals that need to be tested to find an infection of given prevalence with 99% certainty; the curve with circles shows how many need to be tested to give an answer with 95% certainty. With most species, far too few individuals have been tested to make any sure assessment of the frequency of infection.

of picking up a prevalence of 0.5% in a population, a sample size of no fewer than 600 would be required. If this seems an absurdly small prevalence to bother about, we must remember that the incidence of bovine TB in cattle, which instituted the wholesale slaughter of badgers, is nationally about 0.01%. In the south-west 'problem area' it is about 0.05%.

The only way to find such a minimal prevalence is to sample many thousands, just as in the tuberculin testing of cattle. It is impossible to replicate this in a wild population, and so the prevalence of TB in a wild species has never been known. We simply do not know if there is a residual level elsewhere in the environment which could reinfect badgers and other animals; only the badger has been rigorously examined. And *eradication* is only a theoretical possibility.

As if this degree of sampling isn't enough to invalidate the notion, Barrow goes on to say:

The figures relate to simultaneous sampling of all individuals in the sample. However, populations change in numbers or in phenotype, and sampling carried out over a period of time would increase the minimum size of the sample... Secondly, the character sought may not be distributed randomly. This will require larger samples, the size depending on the extent of the clustering.

Coffey's criticism was relentless. MAFF, while admitting that the fox, brown rat and mole are susceptible, hastily pointed out the disease in these species is not progressive. Such intrepidity is based on three positive fox samples out of 126, five rats our of 163, and two moles out of 54 examined... How can the ministry be so confident of its conclusions with such a paucity of statistical evidence?

Neither was Coffey satisfied with the historic fudging. We need to know if badgers were, as seems likely, infected before 1960, when the national herd was riddled with virulent cows. If they are 'highly susceptible' as MAFF assert and as Lord Zuckerman frequently stated in his report, then there seems no way in which they could have avoided infection. In which case, we might ask, how did the ministry ever manage to contain the disease, let alone reduce its incidence over most of Great Britain to what is possibly an irreducible minimum without purulent badgers continually reinfecting the 'clean' cattle? How did badgers elsewhere in Britain manage to cure themselves of the disease? What, in short, happened to badger-to-cow cross-infection in the 1960's? The stock response to these awkward but pertinent questions is a bland 'population density variations'. Coffey responds by stating that while he can accept a variable density of badger populations, his gullibility is stretched a little far when asked to believe that nowhere else in the country are there badgers and cattle living in associations similar to those found, apparently commonly, in Cornwall, Gloucestershire, Avon and Wiltshire. Says Coffey:

Population density variations which are at best pure speculation and at worst mirages in a desert of despair, fail to explain with any conviction these inconsistencies.

Again and again geography enters the story. It no doubt infuriates desk biologists but there are serious regional anomalies which cry out for investigation. Cornwall is the major problem area, it has been since the beginning, and yet there has never been a fieldworker in that county looking specifically at causal factors. Possibly because badger #1 was found in Gloucestershire – certainly another affected area – and this being near to regional headquarters at Bristol, and convenient for London, Woodchester Park on the Cotswold escarpment was chosen as the principal study area. Then, again one presumes, the selective experiments were set up at Thornbury, Avon and Steeple, Dorset – both fairly unusual sites (within reach of Bristol) in that they were bounded by effective barriers preventing rapid recolonisation by badgers. Both these study areas were cleared of badgers (and cattle), and maintained thus by repeated gassing; unfortunately, there was no comparative control study. MAFF have, since the onset of gassing, relied excessively on findings from Gloucestershire, Avon and Dorset.

It wasn't always so. The keenly forgotten Richards' Report, mentioned in Chapter 4, looked specifically at West Penwith near Lands End, and made twelve wide-ranging recommendations which covered: i) stock-proof fencing; ii) synchronised and more regular tuberculin testing in clearly defined areas; iii) the continuation of a 'discriminating standard of interpretation of the test'; iv) further investigation into complement fixation and fluorescent antibody tests; v) the prevalence of TB in pigs and their role in cross-infection/transmission to cattle; vi) the screening of wildlife, especially the badger and the rat; vii) closer checks on in-contact cattle consigned for slaughter; viii) liaison between MAFF vets and meat and health inspectors; ix) much tighter controls on the movement of condemned meat ('We were surprised to find that unfit and condemned meat was moved from a slaughterhouse to a processing plant in an open vehicle. This is a practice we deplore since any accidental spillage constitutes a source of infection to any susceptible animal *en route*'); x) disposal of unchecked possibly infected cattle to knackers' yards and hunt kennels; xi) tighter controls on inter-farm movements of cattle in affected areas, and on movement records; and xii) continuation of disinfection of premises by ministry teams.

No sooner had the badger been put in the dock, and summarily tried with a technique that would not have been out of place in a medieval witch-hunt, than it was pronounced guilty and condemned. Some say a witch-hunt has gone on ever since, yet to this day no-one knows for sure how cattle get TB, or from where.

This dilemma is at the heart of the problem; for it is difficult fighting an unknown enemy. The trials which MAFF carried out, the results of which were taken as a didactic assessment of badger involvement, were a basis for more fieldwork and experiment. As we have just seen, MAFF began objectively, studying the problem reasonably open-mindedly, and trying to analyse the role of the badger.

From 1972 through to 1975, badger samples had been taken both from the south-west problem areas and from clean areas in an attempt to assess the prevalence of the disease in badgers. Soon, though, MAFF were forced to bow to pressure from a powerful and impatient farming lobby.

Experimental work went on alongside operational 'fire-brigade' gassing, but the results were not published until the eighties (see Chapter 10), and the fieldwork still concentrated on Gloucestershire and Dorset, where conditions were different to Cornwall: in Gloucestershire, for some reason still unknown, badgers appear more susceptible to TB than elsewhere; and Dorset, where the disease seems to exist in very small foci, is by no means a problem area of the same degree.

The work by Barrow (on a Nature Conservancy Council post-doctoral fellowship) and MAFF staff in Dorset did not so much determine the badger's guilt, for this had already been decided, as determine its sentence. It was concerned with the epidemiology of bovine TB, and showed that the badger was a susceptible species which could probably act as a maintenance host. Certainly the badger could not be ignored.

In the first three Annual Reports *Bovine Tuberculosis in Badgers*, 'Uncle Maff' was in charge and 'Dealing With The Problem'. By 1980 they had dropped both the chatty style and the confident epithet, replacing it with cold officialese. A much sterner, more defensive report emerged. But even in the very first published in November 1976, MAFF gave involuntary indications of their predicament. Where they should have been Dealing With The Problem, the ministry actually spoke of being 'confronted with the problem of tuberculous badgers', and of having to find 'a solution...in order to obviate the risk to cattle and to assist farmers who were sustaining worrying losses'. While there was nothing wrong with this, as far as it went, more worrying was the next sentence which admitted: 'The Ministry was also concerned to reassure farmers that the problem was being contained...'. Somewhat hypocritically, MAFF, then, as now, sought to justify their campaign against the badger by asserting that not only were they protecting the badger from vengeful farmers taking the law into their own hands but also from the blight of the disease itself.

In truth, farmers have always taken out any wild animal seen as a threat to their livelihoods. If real, few would deny them this right. But threats are often mythical, and farmers being fiercely independent do not often bother about the niceties of acquiring licences (permission) to do what they want on their own farms.

Though there is an increased frequency in Gloucestershire, few badgers have ever been found *suffering* from the disease. A 1968 symposium paper entitled *Mycobacterial Infections in Free-living Wild Animals* by Deans, Rankin and McDiarmid (later to become a long-serving member of MAFF's Consultative Panel) did not mention the species but what was said was interesting:

one might even be justified in assuming that all tuberculosis in free-living wildlife has its origins in man and his domesticated animals... While it is unlikely that mycobacterial infections in free-living wild animals will be a major threat to our agricultural industry, it is necessary that we should...take them into consideration when we are designing management systems.

When the Chairman of the Consultative Panel came to sum-up, he said:

animals, in general, do not suffer from most infections unless they congregate in large groups, and that man by forcing his farm animals into large groups has clearly increased infections among them and in so doing has started up infections in animals outside that would probably not have occurred had he not accumulated animals himself... Man, by his own behaviour, has increased the opportunities for animals to become infected; very frequently, it seems to me, the one thing left out of serious consideration is the behaviour of man himself...

I think it worth remembering that animals may be infected in the laboratory with large concentrations of organisms but they may be difficult to infect under field conditions when presented in small concentration.

After Badger #1, such commonsense became much scarcer. The Chairman also remarked that he too knew 'surgeons drop things from which bacteriologists are expected to derive cultures'!

Still dealing with the problem, MAFF in 1976 went on to describe how it was '*impossible* (my italics) to live-trap all the badgers associated with a breakdown herd'. In consultation with the Universities Federation for Animal Welfare (UFAW), MAFF designed efficient and humane traps ('But the technique proved to be cumbrous and time consuming'). In order to illustrate the inefficiency of cage-trapping, MAFF gave details of two operations; in one, the south Dorset experiment, 'only 33 badgers were caught' over a period of nine and a half months with 42 traps. Concerning the Woodchester Park ecological study – without doubt the most important project yet devised by MAFF on this programme – it is drily stated that 'up to 31 July 1976 one badger, 2 jays and one pheasant were caught in 64 trap-nights'.

MAFF 'concluded that the only satisfactory method of eliminating tuberculous badger colonies was to gas them in their sets basing the method to be used on the technique already available for gassing rabbits in their warrens'. Insisting they were doing the badger a favour they gained the support of various outside organisations. Unfortunately this platitude, exhumed later by Lord Zuckerman, is still trundled out by MAFF parliamentarians in response to MPs' questions.

It is surprising just how many stock MAFF tenets were squeezed into the two initial paragraphs dealing with the problem. Another fallacy still beloved a decade later by senior administrators is the one which advises MPs and their constituents that 'the only practical means of dealing with the problem is to follow the same policy as is practised for cattle; that is to kill those affected and those exposed to infection'. Demonstrably this is exactly what does *not* happen. Cattle are destroyed on reacting to the tuberculin test, in-contacts being slaughtered only in exceptional circumstances. Badgers are not, as yet, diagnostically live-tested, and can be killed on suspicion even where there has been no disease in cattle.

On 7 August 1975 the first badger sets were experimentally gassed. Government departments appear to find public relations rather irksome but MAFF did have a half-hearted stab at it soon afterwards when they demonstrated their gassing technique for the benefit of the TV and press. The winning gas was a cyanogenetic one; carbonmonoxide (less toxic) and the nerve gasses (too dangerous to handle) coming in well behind. Various powdered compounds of cyanide have been used for rabbit destruction since 1900. The powder is driven into the tunnel system by mechanical pumps, where, in contact with moist air, it is converted into hydro-cyanic gas (HCN), more often called hydrogen cyanide.

We may have become used to ministries instituting research *after* they have become committed to policies, but it still seemed strange in 1976 that the highly contentious gassing of a newly protected species was initiated on the strength of methods used traditionally for rabbits – whose underground burrow systems are quite different.

Research into the optimum levels of HCN for badgers began in March 1977, but in 1976, six gassing teams – each consisting of a supervisor and three operators – had already been recruited. Three were for experimental work, the others were deployed in the 'fire-brigade' operational work which began in December 1975 in Avon, Gloucestershire and Wiltshire, and by the following March in Cornwall. By the end of August 1976, there had been 59 fire-brigade operations, a further 53 surveyed, and two more teams had been recruited in order 'to maintain a satisfactory impetus'. In the experimental work in Dorset by 18 April 1976, six hundredweight of dry HCN had been used in 1,898 badger holes, amounting to 247 sets (groups of holes) over a control area of 1,200 hectares.

In Avon by September, 177 sets had been gassed, and it had been found necessary to re-gas on 235 occasions; one set had to be gassed 19 times and repellants used before re-opening by badgers ceased. One year later, 42 more sets had been gassed making a total of 219, amounting to 2,057 holes.

MAFF's 2nd Annual Report, published in December 1977, announced that trials were undertaken by the Pest Infestation Control Laboratory because 'of the lack of information about hydrocyanic gas concentrations in badger sets'. What follows in this report and the next one two years later is further indication of the prevarication that is so often apparent when authority is confronted by unexpected or embarrassing evidence. But should scientific research be anticipating results anyway?

The report admits:

Although the established gassing procedure which has proved satisfactory in general use [*by whom?*] was followed, measurable concentrations of hydrogen cyanide were detected at only 5 sampling points out of 22 in this case. The set was re-gassed the following day, using a greater quantity of powder introduced at 3 entrances. As expected, distribution was better and measurements obtained at an additional 6 points.

The report goes on to indicate

the problems of obtaining a good distribution throughout the set. Nevertheless the treatment appeared to be successful and the bodies of 2 recently-killed badgers...were recovered. Death from inhalation or ingestion of lethal doses of cyanide is the result of a histotoxic anoxia and usually occurs within a few minutes of the cyanide entering the animal.

In 1979, MAFF merely repeated this *verbatim* before going on to describe subsequent trials.

Results...showed that, ten minutes after blowing cyanide powder into this semi-natural set, concentration exceeded 150 parts per million (ppm) at eight [of 20] sampling points... At other points, including several blind ends, the concentrations were low. ...In another test, using a larger quantity of powder, applied at more points...concentrations in excess of 150 ppm were obtained at six of the sampling points...but readings at blind tunnel ends were again low. During a further test, the application of even larger quantities...produced concentrations exceeding 150 ppm at all but one of the sampling points.

The rider 'the use of this high dose technique could be considered on occasions when the normally recommended procedures were not completely effective' suggests it was not an option which was to be used very often.

What a pity that before embarking on a programme destined to kill between ten and twenty thousand badgers in 4,500 sets, no-one bothered to find out whether a concentration of about 150 ppm of HCN was efficient in killing badgers. We shall see later that a humane level for badgers, as opposed to monkeys, cats and dogs, was over twelve times this. Man only believes what he can see and touch, that is why the most extreme examples of his behaviour are committed at one remove from reality, such as in the Arctic, on the high seas, or below ground.

SIX

'I wish I'd never got involved'

He runs along and bites at all he meets

(Clare)

Confronted by mounting public hostility, the Rt Hon Peter Walker MP, Minister of Agriculture, issued a Press Notice on 25 September 1979 in which he expressed his concern 'about the criticism of this Ministry's policy for dealing with badgers infected with bovine tuberculosis, and their role in the epidemiology of the disease in cattle, and on the methods used to eradicate the disease'. In this statement, the minister went on to say that he had therefore asked Lord Zuckerman OM 'to take an objective look at the problem' and advise on 'the way it should be tackled in the future'.

The two men were friends but apart from that two of the reasons why Lord Zuckerman was chosen were his former eminence as a zoologist, and his presidency of both the Zoological Society of London and the Fauna and Flora Preservation Society. It was hoped that this appointment would allay the fears of conservationists and non-vested scientists.

Public wrath was at its greatest in and around the Cotswold Hills. In May 1977, BBC television had screened the highly popular, innovative and excellent 'Badger Watch' series: live film of badgers at the site in Gloucestershire where MAFF scientists were studying their ecology and behaviour. The series 'turned on' many people to the value of badgers and aroused their doubts about the control measures being taken against them. The repercussions increased with the gassing of the stars of the now famous 'beech tree set' soon afterwards. This followed the death of a badger which viewers saw enter and not re-emerge from a little-used hole; next morning, a female badger was found dead just inside the entrance. On post-mortem examination, she was found to have died from TB. The set was doomed.

The *Western Daily Press* in Bristol continued to cover the wider implications of the problem, and had long been critical of MAFF policy. Even in the minds of those involved professionally a large number of doubts existed. Paul Barrow outlines these 'main reasons for concern' in his *fresh look* paper of 1982. They were:

that i) there is concern over the 'open-ended' nature of the present policy and MAFF appears to have no long term policy for control, ii) there appears to be little conclusive evidence that it is the badger alone that is responsible for the infection of cattle, iii) despite the epidemiological associations between the distribution of infected badgers and cattle the true extent of transmission from badgers to cattle is not known, and iv) because there is no method for testing live badgers for infection, large numbers of healthy animals are inevitably killed.

I would add to these a fifth: doubt that TB in cattle is still a problem worthy of drastic measures against a protected, generally beneficial and highly esteemed wild species. Dr Barrow was preparing his work at much the same time as Lord Zuckerman.

Gassing of badgers except where necessary to maintain an already cleared area was suspended on 25 September 1979, the date on which Zuckerman was appointed. A sigh of relief from people in many different walks of life seemed to sweep across the country. This must be the end; the ministry would climb down; it was a far more subtle problem than they had thought; at last they would listen to the voices of protest. The end, in short, could now be seen not to justify the means. In conservation circles, it was felt that the ministry would be asked to monitor and maintain the prevailing low levels, extend their research and development, and recruit the services of more scientists and vets. It would employ skilled fieldworkers to look specifically at local conditions and the regional anomalies which were clearly at the root of the unbalanced spread. It would extend the revolutionary work of Dr Chris Cheeseman at the Woodchester Park ecological project to other more typical areas (less densely populated with badgers), and it would wholeheartedly support research into possible biological controls such as vaccines and live-testing for badgers.

Events were not to transpire thus.

Lord Zuckerman, with commendable speed and in refreshing, simple language, reported within one year. It was an extraordinary report by any standards. With hindsight, it might have been better if he had been given more time, written it in a more formal scientific style, and had actually been objective – as originally requested of him by the minister. However, the objectivity was not missed by Peter Walker, who expressed his gratitude to Lord Zuckerman 'for his masterly assessment of a complex and hitherto controversial subject'.

The report, far from quenching the controversy actually inflamed it to heights not hitherto reached. But before looking at this masterpiece, it behoves us to remember the events which caused its inception.

In August 1979, MAFF announced its intention to gas a set of badgers at Corndon Down on Dartmoor in Devonshire because an infected individual had been found nearby. A massive protest was organised resulting in the formation of the Dartmoor Badgers Protection League (DBPL), which dubbed the social group: 'The Domesday Badgers'. Exactly 900 years ago, as I write, in 1085, ancestors of this ancient family – the Spitchwick Badgers – were being documented in the Domesday Book. Protestors did not accept the slim risk to cattle as sufficient cause to expunge such a living link with the era of William the Conqueror. They demanded, at the very least, proof of the ministry's allegations – proof which MAFF have never been able to provide. It was not just the local commoners, landowners, conservationists and even some farmers who were protesting, it was also the general public, holiday-makers: people from all over the country.

The facade of officialdom sits uneasily on the shoulders of a wilderness that emerged as man trembled in the form of a strange little tree-shrew hiding from Mesozoic dinosaurs. But bureaucracy is not so young its mistakes can be attributed to honest idealism. The face is weary in its cynical youth: to many it looked corrupted by the irreconcilable demands of political paymasters and the desires of society. The ministry could not present the badger as a villain, and indeed, with the exception of a few unguarded remarks by a few jaded stringers, has never really tried to. The badger, suffering in silence, was unable to generate general hostility. The protestors were by no means just the young, they included retired army officers, nobility, academics, politicians, civil servants and the farmers who, of all people, the ministry might have looked to for support.

Questions were asked. Cyanide gas worried the water authorities and those whose memories of wartime atrocities against other persecuted races were far from short. Was it regretted in minds and desk-jotters that badgers slept in chambers unwittingly awaiting their executioners? 'Belsen-orientated gas chambers' as Eric Ashby, the noted film-maker who had taken most of the early footage of wild badgers in the New Forest, called them, tucked away out of sight and regarded by experts in chemical warfare as a pretty fair representation of human fall-out shelters. The campaign would have been easier to sell had the quarry been red in tooth and claw and a menace to young children.

The ministry, though, found justification increasingly difficult; they were truly on the horns of a dilemma. Even their own Consultative Panel (CP), which was set up in 1975 and included experts on badgers, disease and agriculture, appeared as though it was a token to mollify the alarm of objectors and the general public. In this it failed, not because its members were not highly respected but because the minutes of its meetings have never been published and because it was feared that its advice was scarcely heeded unless it happened to fit in with the preconceived plan. Critics pointed, and can still point, to the small print where it is found that the Chairman, Secretary, Chief Veterinary Officer 'and other senior officials of the Ministry also attend Panel meetings'. Ah, there, it was felt, was the rub.

Whatever the truth, it was unknown. Public disquiet and suspicion was not assuaged by this silent team, nor by MAFF's consuming secrecy or their understandable reluctance to get drawn into open debate. Secrecy, except in situations of real national emergency, is only necessary where some doubt exists. The desire to conceal information can give morality a hood.

So, largely as a result of the DBPL and the Cotswold Wildlife Protection Society, Peter Walker declared concern and hired a trouble-shooter. Lord Zuckerman's credentials were certainly impressive; apart from holding the presidency of the two august societies, we were told that he had extensive experience of animals and their welfare. He had been secretary of the Zoological Society of London since 1955 before acceding to the presidency twenty years later, and had been Chief Scientific Adviser to the government. Was he in their pocket? With the keenness of a trusted sheepdog, Phil Drabble rounds on official ineptitude wherever he sees it intruding into country affairs. He was doubtful of Zuckerman – describing him later as a scientist eminent in Churchill's day – and cared not who knew it. Perhaps tremulous Britain needs more frankness from senior and generally esteemed public figures. Tam Dalyell MP in *New Scientist* described him as a figure who had padded round the corridors of power for twenty years.

Most people, however, concerned in the great badger controversy in 1979, even, I dare say, many within MAFF, relaxed with Zuckerman's appointment and turned their attention to other environmental matters. Most were duly impressed by the noble Lord's formidable reputation but the main relief was that gassing had been suspended. Few, I believe, seriously thought it would begin again. The events seemed to be following a well-rehearsed sequence: a face-saving run-down, some economic measure, and the leaders would catch up with the led. After all, the badger had been tried for most of the seventies, was it unreasonable to suppose that it would be either cleared or convicted, and if convicted then a fair sentence passed upon it?

Maybe the optimism was merely wishful-thinking. As publication drew nearer, it diminished to be replaced by a foreboding which was to prove prophetic. On 30 October 1980 a Press Notice emerged from Whitehall Place. In it the minister welcomed Lord Zuckerman's report, displayed general satisfaction with it, and announced that gassing would be resumed in the south-west. He tried to skate round the recommendation that 'further enquiries about cyanide should be made' and that 'the Government's Chemical Defence Establishment be called in...', but agreed 'that an overall review should be conducted at the end

1. The Badger – symbol or slogan?

2. Desecration and death in the countryside. Two badgers, one clearly a female, die for the amusement of man; their earth-fastness laid open.

3. Moments in the death of a
badger (part 1): the hands of men.

4. Moments in the death of a badger (part 2): the tools and dogs of men.

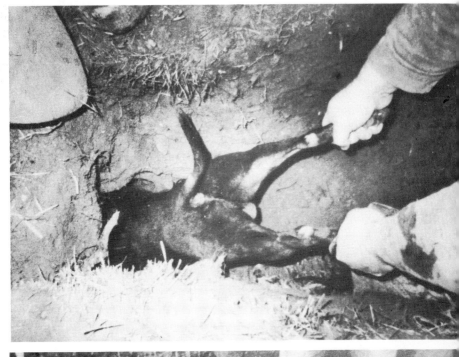

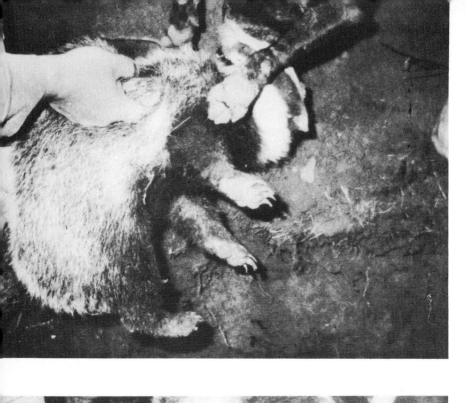

5.(a) (b) Moments in the death of a badger (part 3): the brutalisation. (a) badger trussed up and incapacitated versus at least seven dogs. Note the chain round the hind legs of the badger (see page 78).

(b) this remarkable picture says much about the brutal cowardice of man. The badger pinioned between vicious tongs and perverted dog struggles vainly in the mud for the peace that has been lost forever. The boot is in and the toes the line.

6. Many farmers, even those keeping cattle, enjoy having badgers on their land and give them space. This is an unusual site for a set and indicates a scarcity of ideal habitat.

7. Emerging from its set in a Cornish wood one August evening, this badger (with attendant fly) tests the air for danger.

8.a A badger, suspected of carrying tuberculosis, awaits its fate in a Ministry cage-trap. It has tried ineffectively to dig its way out.

8.b Animal liberation groups directly oppose the agriculture ministry's trapping regime. Here a badger which would have been killed to see if it had tuberculosis is liberated by an unconvinced farmer.

9. A 'Domesday badger' from Dartmoor – scene of the long-running protest campaign which prompted the Zuckerman enquiry.

10. A pair of badger tongs considered quite small by some standards. Pelt of average sized sow for scale.

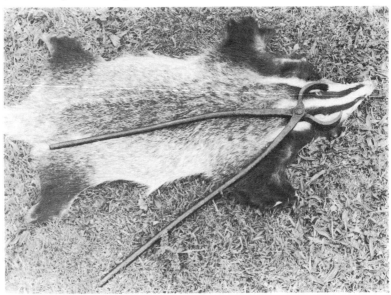

11. Yet another badger falls victim to the most common, wasteful and lethal predator of all. Man kills more badgers with his motor vehicles than in any other way. If found to have bovine tuberculosis, this death could cause many more (see chapter 7).

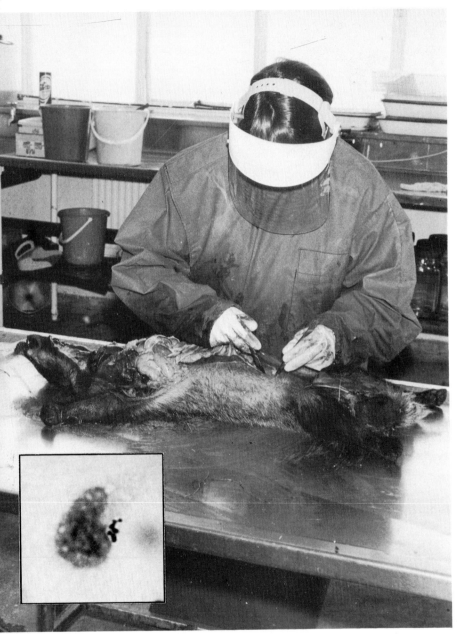

12. Looking for tubercle bacilli (TB). Post-mortem examination of badger by Ministry veterinary surgeon.

Inset: A macrophage containing several phagocytosed acid fast bacilli.

13. Looking for TB and marking live badgers at the Ministry of Agriculture's ecological study in Woodchester Park, Glos., **a)** taking blood sample, **b)** tattooing, **c)** ear-tagging.

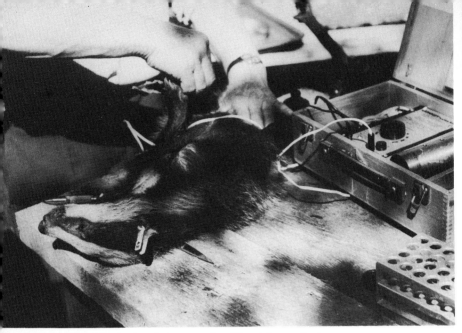

13.c Live badger being tested at Woodchester Park.

14. 'Processed' cub at Woodchester Park in holding-cage prior to release.

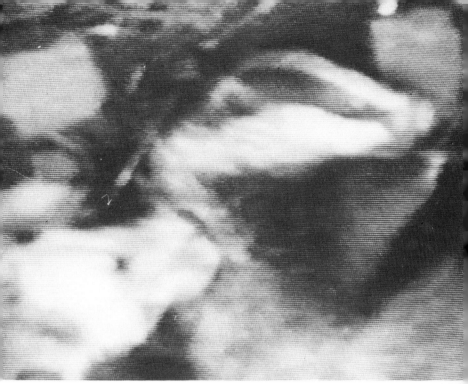

15. Scene from a real life video nasty; a young female badger with no will to fight cowers from enraged dogs and survives torture and torment for three hours before having her skull smashed with a spade. (*Still taken from industrial freeze-frame video recorder*).

16. The public has always opposed official action against the badger. On its tenth anniversary in August 1985 vigils took place all over Britain at the places where dead badgers are examined.

J. Taylor & Son, Northampton   Entered at Stationers' Hall.

17. One of only two photographs believed to exist of the poet John Clare – author of poems printed at the end of the book – taken two years before his death in 1864.

of three years'. The rather bland announcement was reported without demur in the national press – which has never been able really to understand this complex problem.

However, a storm was brewing, and following a short period of post-Zuckerman shock, badger protection groups had to lift themselves, reform and retrench in readiness for the fight they now knew was inevitable. At the same time, critics – lay and scientific – of MAFF's policy were analysing the Zuckerman Report (ZR), and finding to their surprise and consternation no significant difference between the two.

If the report was not exactly whitewash, the feeling was that it was splashed on pretty thickly; all objecting voices were scathingly rebuked or, if eminent, undermined. The NFU were delighted, the scientific fraternity split with the majority aghast at Zuckerman's selection of data, his apparent unquestioning acceptance of them, and their regurgitation in undigested form.

'Lord Z. Under Growing Attack'; 'Scientists Badger Lord Zuckerman Over Gassing'; 'Whitewash'. These are not taken from tabloid newspapers but from specialist journals. The vehement criticism resulted in the extraordinary spectacle of the remote peer and, even more extraordinary, his friend the minister coming out into the open and publishing rebuttals under their own names.

Leading the scientific counter-attack in highly respected journals like *Nature* and *New Scientist* were the prestigious Mammal Society and experts like Dr Hans Kruuk. It was claimed, amongst other things, that the report contained 'biased interpretation of the evidence'; conclusions which were 'too categorical and are not justified from the data presented'; 'factually misleading statements'; 'many anomalies'; and that its recommendations did 'not take sufficient account of the complexity of the problem' nor did it help solve it. *New Scientist* summed up the criticism by suggesting that Zuckerman was 'trying to close the door on an unsolved problem'. Many felt that he was simply defending the ministry: something they could not do themselves in public.

At the same time, independent experts were also having their say. One of the leading figures to do so in the south-west itself Eunice D Overend, who had already published a paper in *Oryx* suggesting that not only was gassing inefficient but since it was not capable of killing each and every badger simultaneously, could actually spread the disease by disrupting uninfected social groups which were then liable to penetration by alienated and usurped infected specimens from disturbed areas. This she considered especially likely during the summer, when outlying sets were difficult to find and if, as had been shown, ill badgers were prone to strange behaviour such as lying up above ground and in buildings.

Much of the objection to MAFF was directed at their gassing

rationale – supported and condoned by Zuckerman. That MAFF now acknowledges it was inhumane, impractical and inefficient does not comfort; they also privately feel it was counter-productive. Yet it was defended indignantly, and so was the notion that TB was rife in badgers, and that they were by extension a hazard to cattle and, therefore, to farmers too.

Lord Zuckerman, showing scant regard for the wisdom of advanced years, leapt aboard this trolley. Throughout his report, MAFF's campaign against the badger was endorsed:

Badgers are *highly susceptible* to the bovine tubercle bacillus, and the resulting infection takes a *virulent* form which encourages the *rapid* spread...; There can be no doubt...that there has been a *significant increase* in the incidence of the disease in badgers...and it is a *highly disturbing* thought that tuberculosis may now be spreading from the dense, *highly-infected* population in the South-West...; What is abundantly clear...is that the problem...concerns...the future of the badger itself... By any epidemiological standards the prevalence of the disease in the badgers of the South-West is *dangerously high*; ...*incontrovertible* evidence that the prevalence rate of TB is *dangerously high*...; we are dealing with a TB prevalence rate...that has already reached *extremely dangerous proportions*; the present level...in the South-West is *very high*...; a TB *epidemic of serious proportions* in badgers...; the disease has now become *very common* in the badgers of the South-West...; ...there is a *serious TB epidemic* in badgers...; ...the *very high* prevalence of tuberculosis in badgers of the South-West...,

and

...an epidemic which...*threatens the local survival* of the badger... (The italics are mine).

Miss Overend, with calm understatement summed up this remarkable hyperbole by saying then all that really needs to be said now even with the benefit of hindsight: 'the evidence for dangerously high prevalence in the south-west is anything but incontrovertible'.

She summarised her criticism by saying that

Lord Zuckerman painted much blacker a picture of the situation than is known to be the case by those actually working on it. This seems partly to be due to a misunderstanding of how the figures quoted by the ministry were obtained... The greatest harm the Report is likely to have done is not so much to the badger (though this is considerable and unwarranted) as to the good relationships being built up between responsible conservationists...and the farmers, who will now have good reason to associate the word 'conservation' with an extreme and antagonistic viewpoint.

In *New Scientist* she is quoted as saying:

The errors in the report are either mistakes, in which case Lord Zuckerman is not the good scientist we thought he was, or they are deliberate, in which case the whole report was conceived to justify MAFF's policy (of gassing badgers).

According to *The Beast* both Eunice Overend and *New Scientist* received 'thinly-veiled threats of legal action'.

In another analysis of the ZR, Dr Derek Pout, an expert veterinary pathologist and surgeon, said:

The report appears to be designed to achieve the following:
  i. Explain how the current situation arose;
 ii. Answer the criticisms of those who protested at the gassing of badgers;
iii. Demonstrate that badgers were responsible for the maintenance and transmission of the disease to cattle;
 iv. Provide a case for the pursuance of MAFF policy in the eradication of infected badgers;
  v. To make recommendations for future action.

Pout was also critical of Zuckerman's method:

In attempting to give a history of the events, educate the reader in matters of pathology and epidemiology, provide experimental evidence, refute criticism and relate personal testimony, as well as push the official MAFF policy, it is not surprising to find confusion in the text. There is therefore a muddled, coercive, patronising and unobjective flavour to the report which makes it difficult to analyse... The format of the ZR provides a useful means of demonstrating how the position on this topic is currently understood and explained by Lord Zuckerman and MAFF... It seems that the ZR accepts that there are anomalies in the association between badgers and cattle breakdowns. The earlier assertion that badgers are 'highly susceptible to the bovine tubercle bacillus' is modified in the statement that 'the members of a species, and indeed any social group within a species, can be expected to vary in their resistance to infection'.

Pout goes on to say:

The sad thing about all these assertions and contradictions is that if a good summary of the complexity of tuberculosis had been given the reader would have been capable of understanding the problem.

In dealing with the prevalance of TB in badgers, Pout observes:

On three occasions the ZR stresses the anonymous opinion that infection rates in badgers are too high, and yet admits that there can be no idea as to what rate is 'safe'.

These criticisms provoked a response, especially those from the Mammal Society, Dr Hans Kruuk of the Institute of Terrestrial Ecology, Phil Drabble in a trenchant article in *The Observer*, and Compassion in World Farming (CIWF) – who accused the government of allowing infective cattle into the country during a strike of Irish vets between November 1974 and June 1976, and that later, with an increasing prevalence in Eire, screening was unable to prevent such imports. It is unlikely that this had no effect on the British incidence of TB.

YEAR	IRISH	BRITISH
1975	0.022	0.002
1976	0.029	0.0007
1977 (Jan–Sept)	0.21	0.0009

Table I. Incidence of tuberculosis in Irish and British bred cattle slaughtered in Britain (expressed as %).

Reports from Ireland suggested that the switching of ear tags and identity cards, enabling reactor cattle to be sold as healthy, was a widespread practice. Whereas MAFF controlled the disposal of reactors in Britain, in Ireland it was left up to the owners, leading to abuses of animal health regulations. The Irish connection was not mentioned in the ZR.

CIWF commented that the report was 'certainly a unique production... Unique...firstly in the omission of certain evidence, and secondly in the conclusion which is diametrically opposed even to what evidence has been collected'.

Lord Zuckerman was obliged to defend himself and his endangered reputation. It was always on the cards, given his high profile as an adroit politician, that the controversy would become acrimonious, and this soon happened – Zuckerman took attacks on his work as a personal slur. Now, several years on, with gassing suspended and admitted by MAFF to have been inefficient, much of the scientific debate of the day is irrelevant. Nevertheless, a rudimentary autopsy of the Zuckerman row shows how dangerous it can be to appoint a single person – especially a politician ('the supreme political scientist' according to *The Beast* 'the magazine which bites back') – to positions of great power on non-political matters.

Lord Zuckerman reserved much of his energy for a diatribe against the Mammal Society; he challenged their competence and even the constitutional right of its elected officers to discuss *contentious issues (relating to the study of mammals) with the aim of showing where more information is needed in order to reduce the uncertainties of the issue*, and yet this was *exactly* the mandate given the Council of the Mammal Society by its membership at its AGM in 1973.

In Zuckerman's opening salvo in *The Sunday Times* of 4th January 1981, he dismisses, without any explanation, as 'nonsense' two main criticisms of MAFF's policy: that there are high densities elsewhere in Great Britain of cattle *and* badgers without any incidence of TB, and that he 'too easily' dismissed the possibility that other animals might be carriers. These two questions remain unanswered. Elsewhere, he speaks of 'the same small company that has always refused to discuss the basic facts' in describing two of the interested parties located in the heart of the south-west problem area who had long been involved and were, in fact, partly responsible for his appointment.

The furore that Stephen Harris, on behalf of the Mammal Society, had started, following his letter in *Nature* on 11th December 1980, was not to be doused by a brief flirtation with the controversy in a national newspaper, and Zuckerman felt his professional reputation sufficiently at risk to take up arms in the scientific press. Unfortunately it did little to lift the allegations of bias for his invective against the Mammal Society got shriller. Lord Zuckerman turned his sights on the credentials of some of the critics of his work, namely Drs Stephen Harris and Hans Kruuk who both, as professional mammalogists specialising in fox and badger behaviour, contributed to the Mammal Society's corporate statement. Even Britain's leading badger expert, on the ministry's own admission, Dr Ernest Neal, was not spared. It became increasingly apparent just how little importance was attached to the natural history of the badger when it came to assessing its role in the epidemiology of a disease of which it was supposed to be the prime carrier. It has long been a criticism from the scientific lobby that veterinary considerations – which see wild animals as property or laboratory subjects – have over-balanced and distorted the issue.

It was surprising that Lord Zuckerman, whose zoological reputation was built on anatomy and the captive behaviour of baboons, saw it as helpful to question the credentials of eminent field-workers and badger experts. 'In its haste to criticize', the corporate statement from this 'quasi-scientific' society was described by Zuckerman as having 'no scientific value', 'irresponsible' and 'wildly astray'. The peer relied to a great extent on one or two allies, one of whom – Dr Frank Yates of the Government's Pest Control Laboratory, Rothampstead – claimed that what the society had done illustrates 'the way in which distorted and partial graphic presentation can be used for propaganda purposes'. An ironic tit-for-tat charge given the ones flying in the other direction ever since the ZR hit the HMSO bookstalls.

After attacking the Mammal Society's constitution, he switched to condescension:

the young Mammal Society has...done itself harm... It might have been more charitable to say that what was done was done out of ignorance. But then, as Gunnar Myrdal has put it, one has to remember that ignorance, like knowledge, can be steered for a purpose.

I was not privy to the not-so-young Mammal Society's deliberations in Council but I would not be surprised had they reacted 'Precisely, my noble Lord!'.

Following Phil Drabble's article in the colour supplement of *The Observer* in September 1981, the minister himself, Peter Walker, felt sufficiently badgered to take, as he put it, 'the rather unusual step of going into print today [in *The Observer*] to counter these critics'. His article was titled, somewhat unfortunately bearing in mind subsequent events, 'Why we have to gas the badgers'.

To students of the problem, his article was disappointing, it contained nothing new and was largely a repetition of official stereotyped responses: much of it, I suppose, to uncharitable minds, capable of being seen as distortions of the truth, and the presentation of partial ignorance steered towards propaganda purposes.

The independent and non-vested scientists had obvious difficulty in convincing the politicians that they alone could be truly objective. The case against the badger was far from proven, and this was and still is the main thrust of their argument. There were plenty of scientists who accepted that the badger could be a risk to cattle under certain circumstances but even they were far from convinced of the efficacy of MAFF's control regime. Hence the theory expressed in Eunice Overend's article 'Does Gassing Spread the Disease?'.

Paragraph by paragraph, Peter Walker's article appeared as complacent, vote-nervous and face-saving stuff designed largely to reassure farmers. It veered from self-defence to the Uncle Maff approach. Maybe one does not get to be a high calibre survivor in Cabinets without the ability to juggle lobbies as vociferous and potentially extreme as animal welfare with one as powerful as farming on one hand, while at the same time saving personal face and departmental pride with the other. The voter is stroked and the seeker after truth alloted his accustomed place.

However, that a Cabinet Minister felt obliged to write a personal article in a national Sunday newspaper defending a government policy that decreed the gassing of a highly popular and protected wild animal, is a measure of the political charge inherent in this debate. Accompanying the article was a picture of a beguiling badger with the caption: 'Badgers' guilt: 'any impartial person would be convinced''. Evidently, that was precisely what had not happened and clearly what was not going to happen.

Of 130 reports and published reactions to the Zuckerman Report in my possession, 66% are hostile; the balance being split equally between support and straight reporting.

SEVEN

When the Gassing had to Stop

The bull dog knows his match and waxes cold

(Clare)

Lord Zuckerman realised the fear that the gassing regime was questionable on humanitarian grounds.

Further enquiries about cyanide should, in my opinion, be made. For one thing, the speed with which cyanide gas kills at different concentrations, while known for a few species has not been determined for badgers. We should find out what concentration in the air of the set would be needed to kill quickly and humanely.

If the hope had been entertained that the whole nasty problem would go away, the generally poor reception which greeted the ZR made this impossible. Quite apart from the immediate furore – the dust of which has never really been allowed to settle – opposition rumbled on throughout 1981 and the first half of 1982. At the by-now-famous Spitchwick set, opposition became more than the bandying of words, slogans and statistics. Things came to a head in August 1981 when on Corndon Common a badger peace-camp was set up with the expressed intention of thwarting MAFF gassing. This camp achieved national attention, and soon provoked violent opposition from some other commoners, who claimed that the tents occupying twenty-five square yards of gorse and rock were depriving them of their grazing rights. Attacks on the protestors forced them to move to adjoining private land, but the vigil continued. Even now, as I write, the Domesday Badgers of Spitchwick refuse to lie down and die.

Eight months after the minister had announced in the House of Commons that to abandon gassing would be 'an act of total irresponsibility', the Chemical Defence Establishment (CDE) at Porton Down, as urged in the ZR all of twenty months before, presented a preliminary report. This resulted in the not exactly common spectacle of Margaret Thatcher's government executing if not a U-turn certainly an adroit 3-pointer. The political risks involved in a government-sponsored slaughter of at least 10,000 of one of Britain's most popular wild animals on shaky evidence were always serious; now, it looked as if the whole operation had been bungled from the outset. The signs were that most of the gassed badgers had died a lingering, agonised death or had been suffocated by the sealed-off entrances. Some certainly would have escaped, and thus lend even more credence to Eunice Overend's fear that gassing actually spread the disease. Neither can we forget that TB is a stress-related disease; the trauma of being half-gassed could not have done a badger's macrophages much good.

The scandal that threatened could have been catastrophic. Peter Walker had to polish his silver tongue. He did it by expressing alarm and surprise, and acting 'at once to suspend gassing as a means of badger control'. The polish he used contained mixtures of the earlier erroneous work, while a deal of elbow grease came from the earlier acquiescence of various welfare bodies including the RSPCA and UFAW which had placed their trust in the government.

Walker said:

These results are unexpected in the present state of informed opinion. They indicate that the response of the badger to cyanide is different from that of other animals such as rabbits. The reasons for this difference are not understood.

The results do however imply that there must be doubt whether all the badgers in a gassed set die quickly and therefore whether they die humanely. This is because the levels of gas secured in a set, on which a report was made to you in 1979, are in general lower than the new experiments show to be required.

These calm words have censored the horror story. What the government's own top-secret Porton Down establishment on Salisbury Plain said was that 2,000 parts per million (ppm) of hydrogen cyanide in the air of the set were needed to kill a badger in about one minute, and that the corresponding figures for five minutes and 25 minutes are 882 and 194 ppm respectively. What Peter Walker was careful not to announce in this statement of 1 July 1982 were the values which were actually set out in the 3rd Annual Report of 1979 to which he alluded. This work, headed 'Chemical Trials on Optimum Levels of Gas' was discussed in Chapter 5, but it can be repeated here that the 150 ppm, considered adequate then and for a further six or seven years, would probably not have resulted in death even after 25 minutes. It is not surprising, therefore, that the 150 ppm hypothesis was left unstated – this concentration which had been assumed 'satisfactory' was underestimated by at least a factor of twelve.

The consequences of this awful blunder to the unfortunate badgers is impossible even to imagine. If we refer back to MAFF's 1977 and 1979 reports, it is clear that the optimum concentration of about 2,000 ppm was scarcely ever achieved under normal operating conditions.

Some saw Peter Walker's statement as 'a courageous about-face for a ministry that had been pumping hydrogen cyanide into badgers' sets for seven years despite protests from conservationists'; others saw it as inevitable. Inevitable or not, the critics, if relieved that gassing was finally over, were furious – particularly with the Consultative Panel – seen increasingly as little more than a sop to armchair conservationists. Ruth Murray, a leading campaigner based on Dartmoor, and one who had long and loud followed her own idiosyncratic line was widely quoted. She singled out the RSPCA for her fiercest criticism. 'They have issued statements saying that gassing was the most humane method available, while in fact it has caused the animals quite horrifying suffering'. Ruth Murray felt that the whole CP should be 'brought to book', and on this she was not alone.

David Coffey lamented the poor research and ventured that 'people in our own (veterinary) profession who supported it are also looking like Charlies'. Coffey was not coming late to the fold, for in his brave 1977 *New Scientist* article, he had declared:

Nobody demands prophetic wisdom. All that can be expected is honesty and integrity. Objectives should not be diluted or confused... It is reasonable to expect the ministry to take the best advice possible. The ministry's consultative panel on badgers and tuberculosis appears to have been constructed mainly with a view to placating naturalists and conservationists. Responsible naturalists and conservationists want scientific conviction not appeasement.

All agreed that viable optimum trials should have been done before the programme began, not after seven years and many thousands of deaths. There had been reports of half-paralysed badgers and of some with their faces and muzzles torn by self-inflicted wounds. Many people believed that ministry policy was callous and negligent – criminally negligent considering it was illegal to 'cruelly ill-treat' badgers. It seems, now, just another indication of the scant respect we pay to all life, save those forms that stand on two legs and speak our language.

Before the CDE report, Dr Derek Pout had researched the 'knowledge of cyanide and its use in gassing badgers', and had come to the conclusion that

MAFF seem to be undertaking this large and continuing operation without immediate knowledge of the consequences, in terms of toxicity to living things. There was no evidence that any government department had made any effort to avail itself of the existing knowledge (and ignorance) of the biological effects of their actions. Furthermore it was recommended by the ZR that improvements must be made in procedure without stating why... It seems that there is a terrible lack of sensitivity on the part of MAFF to the possible results of their actions.

The distrust of anything secret, especially something as potentially sinister as the goings-on behind the barbed-wire and implacable face of Porton Down was hardly alleviated by the report which emerged, for a cover-up was not possible given the wide discrepancy between their optimum levels and those adopted by MAFF. And it was felt, rightly or wrongly, that if the findings alarmed Porton Down scientists, not, as Drabble has put it, known to be squeamish, they should alarm everyone. The toxicological work at CDE had in this case involved 177 female ferrets (mustelids, like the badger) and four badgers. Distrust was further engendered by rumours that Porton Down, under the pretence of developing a painless poison for foxes, as a form of rabies control (which looks like being another exercise in sledgehammer science), were also working on a more efficient badger gas – supposedly being tested on Ministry of Defence land in Scotland. They had, it was feared, latched onto the notion that badger sets approximated reasonably closely human underground fall-out shelters. Maybe a deep-penetrating gas that worked in badger sets would also do very nicely in wartime.

Ernest Neal and, no doubt, other members of the CP welcomed the end of gassing, and favoured its replacement where necessary with cage-trapping. This was not a sentimental view but largely a rational one. Dr Neal, along with other researchers, deplored the waste inherent in the gassing programme – when all evidence was buried underground. Live trapping is selective (and could be much more so had resources initially been put into developing live-test techniques); the badgers killed quickly by shooting yield abundant research and post-mortem material.

So, cage-trapping – once ruled out as too cumbersome, time-consuming and labour intensive became the preferred alternative to gassing and was, in its turn, stoutly defended. The protestors had won a major battle but not, by any means, the campaign.

In August 1982, MAFF circularised to 45 organisations a paper outlining the merits of various methods of killing badgers, including shooting, digging, cage-trapping, snaring, poison baiting, darting and gassing by means other than HCN. After considering submissions by welfare organisations, cage-trapping was soon instituted, to be backed up by snaring where necessary; this was reaffirmed by the CP, which requested that a detailed Code of Practice relating to cage-trapping should be produced. In response to this, MAFF duly published a control manual which included details of the new cage-trapping

Fig 6 (see facing page)
Determination of badger social territories by bait marking. Lettered circles are main sets; large dots indicate latrines; straight lines from main sets go to latrines from which the colour plastic markers were recovered; territorial boundaries are drawn in. Hatched areas are areas where TB occurred in cattle. From a Ministry of Agriculture, Fisheries and Food Survey in Gloucestershire. (*Reproduced with kind permission of Blackwell Scientific Publications Ltd*)

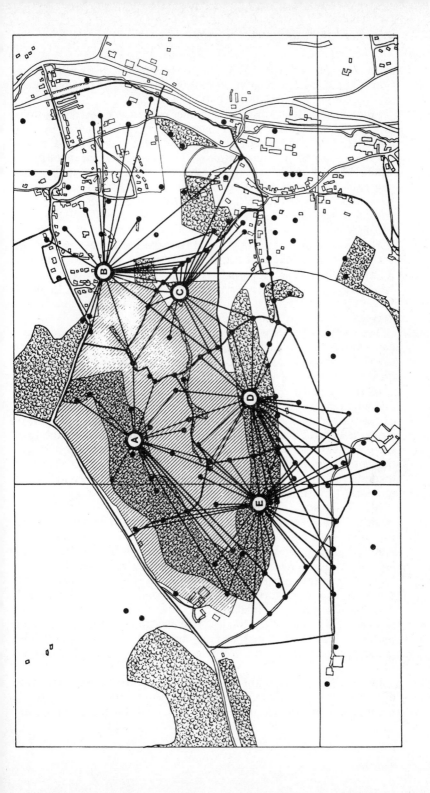

strategies – termed A,B,C,D and E, the preliminary badger investigations (PBI's), badger removal operations (BRO's), and badger social
group determination and elimination techniques.

Since distraught and distressed mother badgers in cages do not suffer
fools gladly, MAFF decided not to trap as a general rule nor snare at all
during the badger's breeding season – which they decided was
February to April inclusive – after it had been pointed out that to do so
would be to condemn badger cubs to wholesale starvation. The
alternative was to examine the trapped animals and release lactating
sows; this continued to be the policy after April, but if MAFF truly
wish to be humane to dependent cubs (if not, why stop at all?) the close-
season should be extended to May.

However, so long as biology seeks to standardise and evaluate nature
with rigid human values, methods and inflexible logic – manipulating
it, in short, into an arbitrary pattern – anomalies will always occur. Dr
Neal gives 8 February as the average birth date for south-west England.
In Cornwall, particularly, births could certainly occur in January, and
very young cubs are common in May.

The trapping policy was, then, refined on humanitarian grounds, it
could hardly have been done on any other for in logic an army does not
shoulder arms and allow its adversary to recruit, nor in disease control
do you stand by and allow your vector to breed.

MAFF is, as David Macdonald put it, 'pinioned by the horns of a
dilemma': even if they wanted to, and by and large they do not, they
cannot persecute the badger as though it were the mosquito, rat or
crow, though their policy suggests it to be more serious than any of
these. Either the case against the badger is *not* after all open and shut, or
the ministry is afraid of public outrage. This vacillation results in
inconsistency and indecision. It was in 1977 that David Coffey
requested 'scientific conviction not appeasement'.

MAFF's post-gassing policy appeased to a certain extent. The new
strategies are a theoretic answer, but they have been heavily criticised
for taking little account of ecological considerations. Natural history
and biological processes, in short, Nature, cannot be caged in human
logic. It is appreciated by all badger experts (few as there are) that our
knowledge of this superficially familiar beast is woefully inadequate;
but we have not yet earned the right to understand any wild animal.
MAFF, determined to finish the job, have felt obliged to try pieces
from other puzzles in their picture. It seems, though, that one or more
pieces are lost, and will be found only by painstaking enquiry. Behind
the grin of the badger lies a host of other factors even less logical than
plodding Mr Brock.

Of MAFF's cage-trapping strategies, A and B are the main ones. One
of these, usually A, is implemented after a farm has suffered a
breakdown and no other likely source is found. From this point on, and

in practice usually much earlier, attention is focussed on the badger. If present on the farm, he becomes the prime suspect and a PBI is initiated. Here, many believe, is the fundamental error.

The case against the badger has been promoted for so long that no-one can be blamed for eyeing it suspiciously, and it is easy to see why some farmers see the badger as a risk they can do without. Farmers, like governments, are reluctant to lose face – they cherish self-assurance – and the badger can become the classic scapegoat, other crimes being heaped upon it. By this time, unless they are very special, farmers' minds are made up. The badger might have been an unsung friend for generations, he might still be an innocent bystander, he might still be a friend – actually protecting farms from outside infection, but by now the 'black spot' is upon him.

MAFF pest officers survey the locale for his signs, and all main and outlier or annex sets which are found are recorded on maps; likewise dung-pits and badger trails. As an aid to delineating territories of badger social groups, a bait containing coloured plastic marker chips is laid: a different colour mixed with peanuts and syrup for each set under investigation. The inert and harmless chips are then found later in badger faeces in dung-pits used to mark by scent the territorial boundaries. Two badgers from each social group encroaching onto the breakdown farm are then usually shot and taken for post-mortem and bacteriological examination.

The work of Paul Barrow, mentioned in Chapter 5, shows how small and rigid this sample is. At least three papers he published in 1982-83 spelt this out. In *New Scientist* of 21 October 1982, Dr Barrow wrote:

If the level of infection is around 13 per cent we would need sample sizes of between 20 and 30 animals to stand a 95 per cent chance of finding at least one infected animal. If however the infection frequency [prevalence] is as low as 2 per cent the number we need shoots up to around 145.

To be 99 per cent certain, that last figure goes up to well over 200. Quite obviously not enough badgers are taken from PBI's to be reasonably certain of discovering a low prevalence. Even more to the point, and this is what Barrow is really driving at, nowhere near enough sampling has gone into estimating prevalence levels in other animals. 'Unfortunately, in some species not even 20 or 30 individuals have been tested.' 'Thus official sampling,' he says in another paper, 'has in no way excluded the possibility of a reservoir of infection in species other than the badger.'

Since 36 badgers would be needed to give a good chance of picking up a 10% TB prevalence, it is easy to see the horns of MAFF's dilemma and sympathise. On one hand it must strive to detect infection while on the other it must avoid killing badgers needlessly. Maybe MAFF has an insoluble problem; if so, perhaps the most sensible thing to do is think laterally and surprise it from an entirely different direction. Unfortunately, the officials charged with this responsibility have never seriously considered this.

If during the course of a PBI, the presence of bovine tubercle bacilli is found (an actively infectious badger is a very rare event), then a 'Strategy A' BRO is implemented, and an attempt is made to catch all badger social groups encroaching onto the affected farm, and all those 'next door' to any in which infection has been found or is found during the course of the BRO. 'This extension of the BRO continues until disease-free social groups are identified and removed (i.e. until a band of non-infected social groups has been identified and removed).' This is the controversial 'clean ring' theory, which can, on the ground, result in a mushrooming operation which extends from territory to territory eventually affecting large tracts of countryside in which badgers are massively exterminated almost irrespective of their disease status. 'And one can imagine,' said Macdonald graphically, 'the chilling possibility of PBI zones developing extensive pseudopodia'. The possibility that an infectious badger has met one from an uninfected neighbouring group, and cross-infected it during a boundary dispute, is said to be the most likely mode of inter-group spread.

This rationale relies on the disease occuring only in certain well-defined pockets, on operatives being able to define accurately all the social groups within them, *and* catch *all* the badgers there. The BROCK Badger Group in Cornwall have monitored ministry activities and have found that MAFF, certainly in Cornwall's admittedly often unusual topography, seem simply to catch as many badgers as they can, and keep this up until they have taken out what they describe as the 'clean ring' – a *cordon sanitaire* – of badgers in which they can find no trace of the pathogen. Critics point out that what lies beyond where the clean ring *was*, is a ring of badgers of *unknown* disease status.

It is equally chilling to some unaffected farmers caught up by these pseudopodia that an equilibrium which has in many cases existed for decades and which is seen to have helped maintain a disease-free herd can be upset by an experimental scheme with unknown side-effects. Once a BRO is considered complete, the area is 'maintained free from badgers for 6 months' – breeding season or not. Again, it is argued that this is much easier said than done, especially in the summer and early autumn, when badgers wander considerably and when they may lie up above ground in dense vegetation.

On small farms, all badger social groups 'encroaching onto the farm' are attacked under *Strategy B;* this procedure then follows that of 'A'. The next strategy is 'C' – this involves a BRO 'without sampling the badger population', and only occurs where there is an endemic problem.

These strategies cover all contingencies following a herd breakdown but it does not stop there. The discovery of an infected badger – usually a road traffic accident (RTA) – in areas of the country with a 'high cattle disease risk' and where bovine TB is an 'established threat to cattle', can result in a *Strategy D*. In other words, BRO's are instigated *without* attendant herd breakdowns. MAFF states: 'After determining the group to which an infected badger belonged, the removal operation follows the same procedure as *Strategy A*'. *Strategy E* is the same except that on 'small farms' the infected group(s), contiguous groups and all other groups encroaching onto the farm are also removed.

These last two strategies appear to ignore certain consideration which could totally invalidate them. Firstly, there is no certain way of 'determining' the origin of an RTA: the badger might have been translocated by animal activists in an attempt to upset ministry calculations and scupper these hotly disputed strategies; secondly, badgers killed illegally are often dumped on roadsides, and though MAFF are strict about not examining illegally-taken badgers, many undoubtedly slip through; thirdly, sick badgers are known to display unusual behaviour, and may even take to scavenging along roadsides, wandering far from home; and fourthly, if the badger is not actually infec*tious* (i.e. excreting the bacilli) – and, as we have said, very few are – it is possible that the road victim is one of the valuable resistant badgers. More of this too later.

Furthermore, the cage-trapping strategies, while a major improvement on the old mass-gassing, could be inoperable, for they depend on the accurate delineation of social groups, and these, once upset, take many years to become re-established – the area in the meantime being used by casual visitors. Later we will even ask if it is desirable to take action against badgers at all. It may be horrifically counter-productive.

The new strategies were initially praised because of the research data they would provide. If the badgers must die – *if* – then at least they would not be totally wasted, not even the healthy ones. On post-mortem examination, MAFF now record details of identification, capture, location, weight/length, age (cub, adult, not known), sex, cause of death, evidence of lesions and lymph nodes (the immune system), and bacteriological results. As a consequence, badgers are divided into three categories: i) cases with visible TB lesions (VL's) and positive on culture of tissues; ii) cases with no visible lesions (NVL's) but positive on culture and iii) negatives – no evidence of bovine TB infection.

On one post-mortem, I witnessed a certain slackness, possibly the result of processing large numbers of badgers; understandable because the badgers were coming through the dissection room in a more or less continuous stream from BRO's and roadsides all over Cornwall. On one occasion, a tissue sample intended for culture slid down the outside of the test-tube, it was dragged back up and deposited inside. The exterior of that tube was then contaminated, possibly with a pathogen, which might then have endangered staff or contaminated other samples in the culture room. Australian work published in 1983 showed how easy it was to spread the disease in laboratory conditions. The words of the Chairman of MAFF's Consultative Panel (see Chapter 5) come to mind.

At the end of the experience, I was aware of the degradation which occurs when a wild animal is crudely extracted from its proper context and analysed as a specimen. It did not help to be told by the veterinary surgeon that really they are pretty nasty animals; although I'm sure no real slur was intended, it seemed indicative of an attitude to wildlife which had more to do with human values than scientific objectivity. Perhaps it was just a defensive response.

The data MAFF is able or willing to collect can be seen to be a very small proportion of that available. This obtained, the carcasses are incinerated. The waste is deplorable even acknowledging the difficulties and limited resources available. The Wildlife Link Badger Working Group in their 1984 report believed that the following at least should be collected: immunological data for research into live-test techniques and the immune response of badgers; data on the reproductive physiology of females, by counting placental scars it would be possible to ascertain reproductive rates of different population densities; more accurate information on the ages of carcasses by reference to material already acquired from Gloucestershire, in this way the age distribution of the disease could be better understood; stomach analyses to discover regional dietary variations and weaning periods; and indication from the adrenal gland, kidney and body weight as to stress levels in the knowledge that TB is a stress-related disease (disturbance to badger infrastructure likely causes increased inter-group aggression which, in turn, may facilitate susceptibility to infection and virulence).

It is not difficult to think of applications unrelated to epidemiology, and researchers in other fields would doubtless appreciate access to such a wealth of unique material, hopefully never to be available again.

EIGHT

Badger in the Tongs (The Fight for Brock)

He drives the crowd and follows at their heels

(Clare)

The plunder of life attributable to the 'countryside muggers' – as Greg Knight MP called them in the House of Commons – just happens to be less in numeric terms than that taken by the Ministry of Agriculture. In qualititive terms, there is little or no comparison unless one contrives to see in both an abuse of wildlife – which belongs to no-one – and the victimisation of a largely inoffensive animal that just happens to be of manifest size.

But there are other unstated links which, however much they are deplored by the authorities, cannot be left unstated if we are to understand the plight of the badger. I have already referred to the justification which the badger tormentors drew from the official action. Some MAFF trappers were recruited from uncertain backgrounds soon after digging was outlawed: gassing badgers was not a job dramatically to reduce the dole queues. Rural cowboys who once pursued the badger for pleasure now possibly had the chance of doing it full-time, on taxpayers' money and behind a crown insignia.

Common fury about premeditated torture and illicit vandalism of a free wild spirit became confused with the cool methodology of a state department. Citizenry feels comfort in the security of such authority. Political expediency is a subject more for TV sit. coms. than real life...until it reaches out and fingers your own collar. The power of the state smoothly persuades.

Farmers, more than most, have a healthy mistrust of bureaucracy, but many have so long been soothed by advice, coerced by grants and flummoxed by contradictory directives they have understandably become if not trusting then dutiful. A consequence of this is the subjugation of independence – otherwise valued highly. To the business farmer, the system becomes a game, played out and exploited; to the more simple, it becomes Big Brother. Rules, like fear, can be real or imagined. I meet a good number of farmers in my work, most thankfully are still characterized by an earthy honesty, but the unwitting mandate assumed by the ministry becomes clear. The simple phrase 'I can't afford to upset 'em' hangs in the air, stated or not. Perhaps the badger sometimes pays the price of that appeasement.

Yet still we must search for the truth. That will be found in the independent, the questioning, the non-vested, the free thinking, and therefore often the young. The badger was seen as something special and that was enough.

It was inevitable that the fight for Brock – which began in a concerted way with the formation of the Frodsham Natural History Society's Badger Group prior to the Badgers Act 1973 – would gather momentum when badger digging was outlawed. In an attempt finally to wipe it out, groups in other problem areas emerged.

Michele Vaughan, founder of the Wirral and Cheshire Badger Group, outlines the early days.

The Frodsham group are much to be admired. Frodsham is a large village built around a hill which has many sets. It is situated on the outskirts of Liverpool and is not far from other industrial areas – Burnley, Wigan, Ellesmere Port, Rochdale etc, – all of which are infamous for badger digging and baiting. The group started because of atrocities at their local and much loved sets. Of course, in pre-legislation days, it was certainly a hard task to stamp out digging even with the help of the police, who cleared diggers away from sets but were virtually powerless to do anything else. I think there were about 75-100 people involved in Frodsham – physically standing guard over the sets, and there were often heated confrontations.

The Gwent Badger Group came into existence soon after the 1973 Act, and were the main inspiration behind the Wirral and Cheshire group in 1979. By this time the Frodsham group had more or less accomplished its task and become fairly inactive, and digging on the Hill had abated.

Michele continues:

Our group began one wet, cold February morning when my local set was badly dug, badgers butchered and I believe small cubs taken. I can't describe the horror or helplessness at finding this large and ancient set so badly desecrated. Of course the diggers had escaped but I felt we couldn't just leave it at that. The local branch of the League Against Cruel Sports kindly offered £200 reward for information on the incident or whereabouts of the cubs. Nothing came to light but several people contacted the newspaper carrying the story/reward and offered help.

We were fortunate in having Jane Ratcliffe living on our doorstep. She had just finished a recording exercise on Wirral, and had discovered that the population had declined by 80% in ten years. Obviously urgent action was needed to retain the small badger population that was left. A small group of keen naturalists formed the nucleus of the group, and we set about listing all known sets, patrolling them, notifying police and local residents of what we were doing. The response was excellent...and we found it best to encourage people to 'adopt a set', gradually we formed the Wirral Badger Group. The TV picked it up, and people from further afield contacted us and we quickly spread into Cheshire... By the end of 1981, most people would ring either ourselves or the police at the first sight of terriermen. They had been getting away with it in previous years because nobody realised what they were doing. We had several prosecutions – mostly successful – and finally we were well established in the study and protection of the species. We appear as 'expert witnesses' for the police, and also are keenly developing a public information service and education themes for young people. We are particularly keen to assist landowners with badger related problems and thankfully enjoy good relations with most parties.

We work closely with the RSPCA, Country Park Rangers and police. It has taken time to convince most folk that we are not extremists or cranks! We certainly discourage the 'vigilante' tag.

In cases where sets were due to be built on, we have successfully negotiated for reserves to be created and sets left alone. I think we created a precedent when we persuaded the local authority to swap a piece of council-owned land for land with a set on it which would otherwise be developed.

This short narrative demonstrates the importance of action and commitment, and provides an object lesson for anyone who feels, no matter how hazily, that we are stewards of the land, never its owners.

In the early seventies, the fight for Brock enjoyed wholehearted public support; it still does in many parts of the country but the Ministry of Agriculture's campaign, soon to begin, in which it was implied or stated that the badger was a threat to cattle, farmers' livelihoods and public health was bound to have an effect. The real threat, it seems, the one to the Exchequer was seldom mentioned.

Those whose personal or professional judgement demanded the truth, found their time consumed in defending the badger's name from mischievous or just plain ignorant statements. Increasingly, discussion about TB in cattle began and ended with the badger. MAFF's annual reports *Bovine Tuberculosis in Badgers* are regrettably titled, for MAFF is not concerned with TB in badgers *per se*. A better title could have been devised – it still could. Back in 1976 there was more doubt around, one subheading ran *TB in badgers and other wildlife*. Now even that could be too restrictive; more objective titles might have been 'Tuberculosis in cattle – environmental factors' or 'Environmental research into bovine tuberculosis' or even 'The role of wildlife in bovine tuberculosis'. The badger could then have found its own due level, however high or low that might be. But pressed by powerful vested lobbies, the badger had already been named, and progressive ecology set about the ears.

Soon after the inception of gassing, it became apparent that MAFF had not got all the answers, and that they had overstated their case. The badger's role as a scapegoat became more prominent. It was certainly being victimised on dubious evidence and, so the fear grew, out of political and bureaucratic expediency. Despite the formation of the Consultative Panel in June 1975 – made up of representatives from interested organisations and expert individuals – a spirited war of words began in place of sensitive and conciliatory science.

Because the minutes of panel meetings are never made public, the fear that its constitution is little more than a sop to conservation should not really surprise anyone. It seems well balanced though rather overburdened with vested interests on both 'sides' some of whose places might be better filled by more detached experts: ecologists, epidemiologists, a biological statistician (to collate and apply the wealth of data already accrued) and a mycobacteriologist.

I can't believe anyone saw the badger as a threat to national security and yet it was subjugated by the Official Secrets Act. To independent observers, the panel became almost irrelevant and a puppet of the ministry. Having found the representative from the main land-using body unaware of how the cage-trapping strategies operated, my own concern is hardly eased. As time went on, the state veterinary service, which is charged with handling this problem – at least bovine TB in cattle – appeared to listen less and less to any advice that countered a policy which had begun, quite correctly, as an experiment – 'something worth looking into' as one professor of zoology described it.

Phil Drabble did more than anyone to bring doubts and fears into the public arena. Here was a naturalist able to speak to farmers and the field sports people in their own language. Rural communities, due to an inherent fear of incomers and usurpers, always were inward-looking. Now, with more and more land owned by fewer and fewer businessmen, we are returning to a quasi-feudal system. The new barons too will fiercely protect their privileges and self-interests. Generally the rural community seems more interested in where a statement comes from than what it is.

Mr Drabble carried the attack to the ministry in a series of audacious statements and articles. Newspapers and other popular media took up the search for justice and were often uncaring for vested interests. Of course the media only like things black and white, and unfortunately the badger issue is about as black and white and grey as its own fur. Again energy was dissipated by defending the badger rather than searching out the truth. Somehow the badger had become the core of the problem.

Things got worse: an absurd position seemed to arise in which organisations spoke out corporately against MAFF policy while their representatives on the CP appeared, due to the British disease, to be going along with it. This culminated in the production of the Wildlife

Link Badger Working Group's report published in late 1984 specifically for the 'son-of-Zuckerman' enquiry, headed by Professor George Dunnet of the University of Aberdeen. It received universal acclaim – even from within the ministry, though it strongly criticised their policy – and made no fewer than 25 recommendations for improvement. Yet nearly half the members of the working group were also ministry advisers.

Such little faith has been attached to ministry impartiality over the years that environmentalists showed less and less inclination to stand idly by and condone badger killing so soon after the species had received a measure of protection. MAFF press statements, reports and official responses to legitimate enquiries, usually direct from MPs, suggested inflexibility and prejudice; the attitude, moreover, was often strangely out of accord with unguarded statements and the obviously concerned disposition of conscientious staff.

But this could not be a laid-back academic debate – for it was conducted beneath a cloud of crisis with nearly a hundred herd of cattle still affected, and a thousand badgers dying each year. The time for this had been following the Richards' Report during the seventies when all bar one of the major battles had been won in the bold, yet always controlled, scheme of Attestation. MAFF's reputation was riding high. There was just one remaining pocket of resistance – time to assess the battlefield using the experience amassed during the preceding years. Instead, an enemy position was sighted and because of political anxiety, an all-out frontal attack was launched. The anxiety led to heavyweight tactics careless of the nature of the terrain, the resistance and the morality.

So, from inexplicable biological resistance – the consequence of still poorly understood epidemology, and no-one's fault – civil opposition emerged. This may have been counter-productive; it is said to have merely hardened the official line but it was inevitable and any suggestion of impropriety obviously fed it.

The Badgers Act 1973, full of good intentions, became almost an embarrassment, except to those it was supposed to curb – who saw it as a goad and were encouraged by the official action. The lawmakers legislated round it and the public were thoroughly confused. Was the badger a goody or not?

Some badger groups grew up as a result – the increasingly complex and convoluted subject and all the political ramifications demanded a specialist approach. Most concentrated on the nationwide, though pocketed, illegal threat with at least the moral weight of the law behind them. Only in that other pocket, the south-west, did groups feel isolated: up against the resources and obdurate might of a government department; a soured farming community (some of whom claimed to have long seen the badger as a threat); vets with divided loyalties; and a general public which, if not apathetic, was subservient to authority or made suspicious by an offical campaign which played on the disease threat to cattle and badgers themselves – nor even shied away from the old spectre of human TB.

Badger digging was ingrained in those parts of the industrial countryside where men had long dug for a living: South Wales, Yorkshire, Nottingham and the County of Durham. But any large conurbation contains its cowards, sadists and perverts, some of whom feed on the tradition of working dogs, and are encouraged by gambling.

In the rural areas, where dignity and respect are granted animals only on man's own terms, badgers have been abused by cruel and stupid men from the combes and moors of the south-west, the gwyles of Dorset and the valleys of South Wales to the dales of Cumbria and Yorkshire, and the ghylls and denes of the north-east; even in the cloughs of Cheshire and the green and pleasant spinneys of Surrey.

In these places badger groups appeared to meet the threat. Some achieved charitable status, though this is difficult if political lobbying to change government policy is involved. In most parts of Britain, the badger groups can rely on the co-operation of others though this may be only reluctantly given or withheld altogether by the fox-hunting fraternity, who perceive a clash of interests. Though legitimate fieldsports claim not to recognise badger digging as a sport, ranks under pressure from a common foe will close like a gintrap. Foxes often breed in badger sets, certainly disused ones, and will go to ground therein; sets are stopped along with earth to help prevent this, and a badger dig was (and still is?) not only a way of rounding-off a foxhunt but also a convenient way of relieving the frustation caused by the *coitus interruptus* of an abortive one.

Tony Crittenden, a Chief Inspector with the RSPCA in Lancashire has been involved in badger protection for some time. He knows the hard work of detection and the frustration of prosecution, yet asks how can it be that the badger still suffers from malicious persecution? He decides:

The main reason is that legislation must be seen to work. It is hoped that it has an educative role... It must also act as an example to others. When penalties are imposed by the courts upon offenders, it acts as a deterrent to others similarly pre-disposed. This cannot happen until an offence is detected and the perpetrators are found. As with much wildlife legislation, the very nature of the badger makes it remote enough for continued observation to be difficult by those wishing to protect it. The most obvious result is that in most cases badger digging is discovered days, or even weeks, after the culprits have gone. The numbers of prosecutions before the courts is therefore but the 'tip of the iceberg' and by no means reflects the true picture of persecution.

Personally, I would like to see badger groups widen their vision to include other cruelly abused and misunderstood wildlife, from frogs to foxes. The Plymouth Wildlife Group, run under the auspices of the RSCPA, looks after the interests of deer, foxes and oiled seabirds as well as badgers, and points the way towards a more diverse and caring movement. Compassion must not fall into that yawning trap of selectivity: in which cruelty is evaluated by reference to some scale of rarity, or the popularity of the species to which an animal just happens to belong – human, fox or lobster. It is cruelty alone that is the growth on the face of man, and only time can judge its malignancy. To relate cruelty to species is to impose a value judgement which merely reflects our own prejudices.

Ecology is egalitarian, and there is a very real need for local action, I would say for vigilante groups on guard for environmental abuse and able to respond immediately. Is it any longer enough (if it ever was) to pay an annual subscription to a large society and sit back with conscience salved awaiting the glossy periodical? That is vital too but the easy part; there is a crying need to protect physically our wild heritage from all the various agencies working against it – hard, unglamorous and uncomfortable work for which one can expect ridicule, abuse or patronisation. But the ecological awareness which slumbers all around is beginning to be mobilised, marketed and more outspoken. In combating the apathy, conservation will become vigorous, radical and sometimes more militant, which is fine so long as enthusiasm and policy is tempered with knowledge, insight and objectivity. David Bellamy and Phil Drabble fight their own battles in their own ways caring little for the feathers they ruffle along the way; the youth needs leaders such as these.

Emotional impulses seem often to be the spur but the sentiment must be creatively directed. It would be easy for over-emotion to favour badgers and ignore, say, frogs. I like to think that my own concern for the badger in its predicament, notwithstanding its 'special place' in Britain's consciousness, would be no more nor less were it a shrew or a slow-worm.

The majority of badger groups which were formed in the seventies and early eighties were responsible and mercifully objective, this was especially so in those battling the illegal persecution and cruelty. There was little need to resort to hysteria – people were already outraged.

Following the example of Frodsham and with moral support coming from the Badgers Act, the Gwent Badger Group was formed and remains one of the most respected. 'There is no room in our ranks for over-emotional attitudes,' they say in their booklet *Briefly on Badgers* which circulates in all badger groups. In addition to publishing literature, the Gwent group also produced a film for *Open Space* – the TV slot created by the BBC TV Communities Programmes Department.

To be fair, in the south-west of England, badger protectionists have a much harder task, for they perceive an additional adversary, and one which hasn't just got the law on its side but is actually, with Crown exemption, above it. Affronted or unconvinced land-owners can do nothing to prevent the Ministry of Agriculture coming on their land and killing the badgers which live there. Others, of course, for whatever reason, acquiesce or actively encourage them – a few certainly see MAFF as a convenient way of getting rid of their badgers legally. Confronted by this kind of double-standard and a monolithic steadfast bureaucracy, there is a great temptation to go over the top, and one or two individuals have succumbed to this temptation.

Lord Zuckerman evidently placed Ruth Murray in this category, for he devoted a quite disproportionate amount of supposedly scientific space – two solid pages in one place – to castigating her personally. If he had found Mrs Murray's evidence unconvincing he should surely have quietly dismissed it and not used his privileged position to enter into what seemed to many like a personal feud and character assassination. Unfortunately, Lord Zuckerman gave the impression of denigrating all evidence, groups and personalities which were not to his liking irrespective of their credentials. Ruth Murray has over 25 years of experience and a legitimate point of view which deserved positive regard. As it was, she saw the need to issue a press statement on 4 November 1980, on the publication of the ZR. This included the following passage:

From the moment of Lord Zuckerman's arrival for the interview he stated clearly that he concurred fully with the Ministry's policy against the badger. Since Lord Zuckerman had been called in as an independent scientist to take 'an objective view' of the situation, before presenting a report to the Minister, the Right Honourable Peter Walker, I expressed surprise and disapproval that Lord Zuckerman should be stating that he was already convinced that the Ministry was right, *prior* to considering all the evidence from all parties.

The interview...developed along lines which had little to do with a sensible exchange of scientific views and it became apparent that the main purpose of Lord Zuckerman's visit was to persuade me that I should endorse the Ministry's policy and retract my opinions and conclusions based on the findings of research instigated by myself since 1955. The heated discussions which took place on 9th April demonstrated to me that there was no useful purpose whatsoever in presenting (him with) my scientific evidence, some of it as yet unpublished data...

Lord Zuckerman outlined the advice and proposals he intended to present to the Minister and there was no question in my opinion, of influencing (his) conclusions which had been made already, before correlation of all evidence.

On the other side, Lord Zuckerman no doubt considered it a pity that if Ruth Murray had sound evidence, she did not publish so that other scientists apart from himself could have the opportuniy of examining it.

Opposition to MAFF's policy has not just come from pressure

groups. Throughout these pages, reference has been made to criticisms emanating from all manner of sources. Mainly the debate has quite correctly been conducted in the pages of scientific and technical journals but frustration has boiled over onto the streets. A particularly nasty and violent incident taking place at Folkington in Suffolk during an experimental clearance operation which resulted in the wasted deaths of over thirty badgers before local opposition caused MAFF to withdraw and abandon their exercise.

Even farmers who might have been expected to support 'their' ministry have sometimes been suspicious and obstructive. One letter from an affected farmer written during the gassing campaign finishes: 'as soon as they left I opened up the set to let the gas out'.

Now, in one way or another, the badger is trapped in the British countryside, and we must ask ourselves why it seems to have no escape.

NINE

Rural Terrorism

He falls as dead and kicked by boys and men

(Clare)

Once stupidity could hide behind ignorance and be excused by custom. The witch-hunts of the Middle Ages; the cruel injustice inflicted on anything unusual, not understood or regarded as a threat can be attributed to fear and superstition. Today, society still discriminates against the extraordinary, the outcast and the oddball – feeling threatened by anything that refuses to fit compliantly into an appointed slot. It expresses this fear with a nervous and aggressive reaction familiar to any animal behaviourist. You do not need to be an ethologist to understand Jane Goodall's accounts of chimpanzee behaviour, and see their human parallels.

What I cannot understand is the gulf that exists between pity and mercilessness, between need and gratuity in the human breast. Most people are neither exceptionally clever nor preposterously dull, and yet we lurch between extreme behaviour and prejudice, unable to control it.

Basic rural communities are suspicious and resentful of urban domination, and the modern world they feel excluded from. High technology teases but alienates them. They are subject to low wages, unemployment, boredom and mechanisation (fear of labour redundancy). There is a growing estrangement from the soil, and in their enviousness, some lash out with bluster, crudity and violence, and seek solace in a bloody-minded return to old prejudices. Clearly the countryside is not immune from the problems of the inner city.

To kill for *pleasure* should not be confused with need or survival. The violence of field sports is scarcely concealed behind an impeccable image of respectability or one of sturdy yeomanry. The upper echelons of this masonry conform to an ethical code; they may be self-appointed arbitrators of their consciences; they may elect themselves to evaluate, and justify their role as countryside governors but most are happy to admit they exploit it for pleasure.

Respect for wildlife – animate or not – is not a traditional part of the rural labourer's or working farmer's creed. How could it be when, during the taming of the land, nature was, for good sound reasons, always the enemy – threatening to pounce on the unsuspecting or careless? It was once a worthy contest which occupied men, women and even children all the days of their lives. God was praised, nature cursed. Most would have known little of social conflicts or wars. It was nature who opposed with its elemental power, wild carnivorous animals and invisible, inexplicable diseases. And, of course, there is still a need today to stanch nature's challenge.

But now, in a countryside evermore sanitized and standardized, we – so recently the prey really – conceal insecurity with aggression. The prime needs of survival – filling the belly, and saving the child – have been wrested from our hands by others for whom the battle with nature has become 'a tradition' (an innate response).

Man, once *forced* to hunt, came to take pleasure in chasing and killing, and invented his excuses. Now, some at least, struggle with their consciences. And now, for the first time ever, we have a future monarch to whom the chase and killing may not be second nature. In no way can the full significance of this have yet dawned upon us.

The badger could neither be convincingly vilified nor honoured. It was an unexciting twilit figure unable to flee and therefore of no interest to the galloping diurnal sportsman. It thus became the property of the labourer: widespread enough to be accessible but a goad in that it had literally to be dug out. And what to do with it once you'd got it? The dog, long a tool of man, was by now inexorably linked to his desires and passions.

Since modern man, unlike his ancestors, chases and kills from a safe distance with modern weaponry, and is in little danger save perhaps from horses and tottering peers, and since I will introduce voyeurism, the question of 'manliness' is invoked. It should not go unnoticed that the masculine pronoun is used throughout and that all but an insignificant proportion of hunters, shooters and fishers are male either by chromosome or inclination.

What is it about the 'He' psyche that clamours for this most extreme form of domination? Surely it cannot just be the vestiges of the primitive hunter – the noble savage ethic? Could not a less absurd rationale be the expression of blatant profligacy refined by the demands of social etiquette and the cult of civilisation? A conquest, if it is to be satisfying, requires at least three elements: an attractive target, a chase and a climax. Lust, pursuit and domination are all historically masculine precepts.

It can be noted here that 'the thrill of the chase' is applicable to animal and woman, and that 'lust' can be for blood or sex or both. So is the pursuit of a weaker individual by a stronger, unless it is for food, clothing or in self-defence, a crime of passion or a passion perverted?

Whatever spurs the adrenalin there is no doubting the positive contribution of bloodsports in the shaping of our countryside: like it or not, we could be much the poorer – great estate, clean river, small coppice, beast, bird and bug. Nor might we have many of our best and most powerful conservationists or a great lobby of young children growing up ready to resist concrete and agricultural desertification.

The tragedy of the badger is that it is neither pest nor impressively rare; neither noble nor ignoble; and neither ugly nor desirable; in short, it has no tradition protecting it nor even yielding it grudging respect. It must look after itself, for there is no etiquette protecting its tenure of the land. Were it a pest rather than a medium-sized lumbering mustelid, it would certainly be more populous and better able to withstand our dual challenge.

The League Against Cruel Sports has demonstrated the link between the fox hunting, which we still condone, and the badger hunting which we do not. We must ask if the motivation of the privileged and protected is not, at its heart, the same as that of the peasant? Can we be sure that the exposed, fleeing and 'naked' fox does not stir exactly the same hormone beneath both the pink garb and the red neck?

The law that granted scant protection to the badger ironically heralded an uncertain era of insecurity. The return to brutality probably does reflect a general malaise of social inequality, recession and bankrupt spirituality, but no longer can the unfortunate exile hide behind myth. Television has forced consciousness on even those who would deny it: the pleasures come at unwitting cost. And just as the thief's morality is bankrupt because he cannot see that in stealing someone *else's* possession he is actually stealing from himself, so to sneer at civilisation while accepting its trinkets is to abrogate the responsibility that is incumbent upon the civilised; and is again theft.

Today's poacher is not the likeable rogue – the lone wolf with a heart of gold dependent on his fieldcraft – he is a cynical and cold-blooded entrepreneur. In Britain. sadly, the green mantle has become, in places, far from pleasant, it can conceal a dark and malevolent heart. The rural thug has perverted crudity into toughness, cruelty into strength, bullying into machoism, cowardice into camaraderie, and sadism into sport. He makes no pretence at respect for his quarry – he despises it. A badger's head turned up on the doorstep of a newspaper office in Plymouth with a note which read 'You can't catch us all'.

The gangs these characters form are furtive, nervy and difficult to infiltrate because they are as cliquey as a gentlemen's club and demand lifelong allegiance. The jealousy inherent in such a sick and mean association is fuelled by mutual distrust. Many of the gangs are from city backstreets, and are comprised of the worst kind of 'countrymen' – embittered exiles and urban cowboys.

There is a now infamous video: three hours condensed into 57 minutes of mind-crushing, vicious sadism. Given the revolting visual spectacle of a wretched young female badger being relentlessly savaged by a pack of crazed dogs, before finally being finished off with a spade, the soundtrack is curiously worse. These are not shame-faced perverts wracked with guilt in dirty mackintoshes, this is group sadism. Betting may be an incentive, so might 'working the dogs', but the prurience is enjoyed – of that there is no doubt. The gloating, the giggles and the gasps of pleasure testify as much.

Man, relieved by group co-operation of the incessant struggle to survive, substituted artifice and group spectacle. The struggle became entertainment – stage-managed as competition in arena, pit and ring; on the platform, stage, track, pitch and television set. Groups behave in a way which maybe alone none of their component parts would: the monster feeds on itself. Maybe, throughout our short history, the dynamics which can build beauty or destroy it are no more nor less than an expression of terrible insecurity. For take away our scheming, our weapons and armour, and certainly our clothes – we are defenceless, harmless and ridiculous. Remove culture too and man, unless he is fortunate enough to be truly simple, must rely on deceit and pretence.

The video is testimony to the inadequacy and cowardice of these time-warped cardboard heroes, and yet it has nauseated all, save the sick in mind, who have seen it, including the Home Secretary, and police chiefs well primed on all manner of violent nasties. Is it inevitable that the sophisticated technology and micro-wizardy which can produce trinket-wonders like the video recorder will goad a brutish reaction in minds too dense ever to comprehend fineness? And that two extremes of human endeavour should merge on the video tape – one assimilating the other?

The baiting and the digging of the badger are linked inextricably. To some, the latter is sufficient but usually it is a prelude to the main event. Both are relics from a dark age. John Clare's poem shows its recent social acceptance, foisted no doubt by fear and hatred. Children at country fairs were long fed on the spectacle of chained and dejected badgers fighting for their lives against relentless terriers. Often these badgers were obtained by digging or netting – which were sports in themselves; baiting was and still is an excess of digging but the badger is always baited underground whether it can be seen or not. Dogs are always centre stage.

A favourite time for digging is when a sow has her cubs about her because then she will be particularly aggressive in their defence. When introduced into sets, dogs are sometimes fitted with electronic tracking devices on their collars in another perversion of progress, but traditionally a measure of skill existed as men were guided by the position and pitch of the dogs' barking. Below ground, the badger will retreat or attempt vainly to escape by digging before turning to face its adversary. When a badger is engaged, the bark changes and the dig begins. Tony Crittenden describes the process:

The degree to which the dig is pursued varies with the type of the set and its location. Large deep sets, or sets in rocky areas are virtually impossible to work and many terriers are lost... In most cases the 'sport' is not solely the intention of killing a badger but the excitement of 'working' the terriers. The tenacity and success of a terrier is a source of pride to the owner, and also enhances the value of the dog and any of its pups. The illegality of the sport does not deter men from areas where 'badgering' is traditional. I have been told by *reformed* badger diggers that 'it only adds to the excitement'...

Digging down to a badger may be a simple job or may last several hours. I have seen shafts of over six feet reaching down to the passages below. The exposed badger is then 'tailed' – that is lifted by the tail and at the same time shaken to prevent it reaching up to bite its assailant. It can then be bagged and removed to another area for further sport.

Sometimes, long-handled badger-tongs with sharp teeth — illegal since the 1973 Act — are used to extract the badger, which may then be, as the Gwent Badger Group say,

prepared, by being subjected to the most disgusting cruelties. These include cutting away or breaking the lower jaw, fracturing the skull, extracting the teeth and removing the eyes and claws. Such treatment ensures that the badger has no chance of matching the dogs which are now set upon it. One photograph in possession of the Gwent Badger Group shows seven dogs attacking a sow which has a chain attached to her hind leg. Whenever she appeared to be getting the better of the dogs, this chain was pulled by one of the diggers, so exposing her vulnerable underside.

A badger which has not been maimed in these ways could hold its own against many dogs, particularly when it is a sow defending her young. One case on record tells of a sow, which, when pulled from her set, promptly broke off the fight with the dogs and dashed back to save her single cub. She carried it in her mouth for a quarter of a mile to another set which was too rocky to dig. This sow, despite being savaged by as many as nine dogs, refused to desert her cub...

Badger-baiting, prior to its outlawing 150 years ago, often involved staking a badger to the floor by its tail and setting dog after dog upon it until it died from wounds or exhaustion. Another method was to chain the unfortunate beast in a barrel; dogs were then put in to drag it out. It was usual to bet on individual dogs to discover the most successful. Old written records of such baiting sessions refer to badgers sometimes having to face a succession of over thirty dogs. The badgers always eventually lost...

A more bizarre method was to take the badger into a town or village, set it free and then chase it with dogs and clubs. The animal was beaten unconscious and then allowed to recover before the process was repeated.

Crittenden continues:

Alternatively, it can be re-introduced to the set for the sport to continue. In the majority of cases, the unfortunate badger is brutally beaten with spades or crowbars to render it senseless when it is then thrown to the dogs for them to 'worry' as a reward.

The injuries and suffering to both terriers and badgers can be quite horrific... Further, it is my experience that serious wounds on the dogs are treated at home by the owner without any reference to a veterinary surgeon – many dogs are crudely stitched up.

This, in itself, is an offence.

It is clear that glory is reflected from the dogs to the owner; and the competitiveness of gregarious man is expressed by gambling. The illegality has forced the perpetrators underground too: pub cellars, remote farms and furniture vans; contact is now largely covert in pubs and at working terrier shows. Occasionally the mycelium is exposed and one is aware for a while of this sordid world. Working terrier clubs exist nationally and there is no doubt they are used by the criminal element. Now and again, a carelessly worded advertisement slips through and consciousness is pricked. One I have from a 1984 West Country newspaper reads: 'JACK RUSSELL Puppies, super litter, very small, well-marked, grand parents, dead game, fox, badger, otter...'. The Patterdale terrier too is popular.

Even more overtly are people sometimes encouraged to break the law such as in the book *The Complete Jack Russell* by D Brian Plummer which has a detailed chapter called 'The Badger as a Quarry'. According to Tony Crittenden, the book is in heavy demand from local libraries, and this particular chapter 'is obviously well read'.

Crittenden, however, continues his narrative and describes the wretched fate of many badgers.

The badger injuries sustained during the fighting are equally severe [as the dogs] and if the badger escapes, wounds which may become infected or, in summer, infested with fly larvae, may cause it to suffer a lingering death. Where the badger is killed, the manner of its despatch is not without considerable pain and suffering.

The following are extracts from a veterinary post-mortem on two badgers found at a set dug in Cheshire:

The badger had evidence of severe trauma to the top of the head, which had resulted in the nuchal crest being fractured and extensive haemorrhages on the ventral surface of the brain. The changes seen are compatible with two severe blows with a blunt instrument... The second animal showed a compression injury around the chest and the immediate cause of death was a ruptured liver which had resulted in extensive internal haemorrhage. The front leg showed a fracture in the region of the elbow. There was bruising to the right hind leg, evidence of a blow to the head, with haemorrhage on the ventral aspect of the brain.

'The culprits were never caught,' says Crittenden.

Is it any wonder, confronted by such crude evil, that people who get involved *on the ground* become angry and frustrated by the apparent apathy of society? Is it any wonder that animal rights groups are becoming more militant, and taking the law into *their* hands? This is not an idle business, we can no longer sit back and hope for the best.

The disinterest is not hard to find. A member of the Clwyd Badger Group, talking to a group of bird-watchers, found out that they had recently 'walked past diggers and their bloodied dogs at one of our worst hit areas. 'Oh, so that's what they were up to', was the comment.'

TEN

The Politics of Science

Then starts and grins and drives the crowd agen
(Clare)

'Scientific conviction not appeasement,' said David Coffey, and these words keep recurring to me. What is the chance of scientific conviction? The controversy surrounding badgers and bovine tuberculosis has done objective rational science no good whatever.

What a curious irrational beast the badger is, and how deeply ingrained it is in our landwise conscience. For centuries it has been prey to our fears and mistrust. Those who comprehend it as an adversary have feared it and have often reacted with violence in the way that most animals do when nervous. We have also been bewitched: the spell woven round scientists and laymen both.

The hardest attitude prevails in the veterinary establishment. They sit uneasily between science and commerce, between animal welfare and animal exploitation. The establishment refuses to discuss the badger issue; a few fearless voices speak out. The system corrupts the love that prompted the vocation in the hearts of the young. Dr Pout's criticism of the Zuckerman Report was published under 'Viewpoint' in *The Veterinary Record* (12 December 1981) so it 'escaped' the scientific bibliography. Instead of answering his pertinent questions, the British Veterinary Association (BVA) answered their own.

No matter how hard their training might try to suppress it, scientists are prey to emotion. The coming-of-age of ecology and the growth of ethology have taken scientists out into the field where they have been confronted not by textbook or laboratory imagery but by nature in all its contradictory perplexities, where fauna and flora shape and are shaped by each other and the coincidence of place.

The scientist who actually goes out and *touches* nature can be touched in return though his heart must be receptive. It is altogether too superficial to believe that it is just the badger's appearance and inoffensiveness which captivates all who touch it.

Specialism inevitably works against ecology as it does any conspectus; few are able to keep in focus a whole panorama. There are many incentives to specialise. We can examine a particular of life or scan the horizon, but it needs a very special kind of camera to focus on a minutium while retaining a depth of field to infinity and an arc wide and free of distortion. There is in consequence an intricacy of views; a complexity of theories, hypotheses and 'facts' surrounding and obscuring the badger.

Usually view is governed by stance, aspect and the physics of sight. It is one function of any researcher or seeker after 'scientific conviction' to assess the assessors that have gone before – to look behind the face – as well as the evidence. Narrow fields of vision, though they may pierce, are, the more laser-like they become, more resistant to lateral influence. A battery of searchlights can illuminate a scene but they depend on synthesis and control; the viewer becomes a surveyor, influenced by the available light.

In any grey area of nature the far-sighted ecologist deserves the greatest respect. We should not forget that *Mycobacterium bovis* is a natural phenomenon *not* a disease, though it might occasionally cause one – at which time it becomes a curb on populations. We have never been told whether the eradication campaign appropriates the organism or just the disease.

If the scanning ecologist can, at the same time, search for the heart of a part then he or she is beyond value. The ecologist holds the key to this case (as most) but whether he will be allowed to unlock it is doubtful. He who holds such weighty keys may not have the power to control them. This is a tragedy of our time. To answer 'The politician' to the question 'Who controls the key?' is much too glib. The politician is not so much the puppeteer as a mere string made visible by some deficient backstage manipulator.

There are many strings in any performance, the more complex, the more there are. The more strings, the more temptation for more fingers. The longer running the drama, the more involved the fingers; the more involved, the greater the personal stake. And the greater the stake, the more self-conscious and the less detached. If one is caught up backstage, there is no way forward to see the production.

As the years went by, and the badgers in our drama died, the crowd grew, and grew more critical, until such time as the producers heard the uproar through their heavy props. The production we witness was staged by the ministry, directed by the administrative vets and sponsored by the taxpayer. But it was put on in a rush with actors rehearsing in the footlight glare. Not only was this inappropriate to the convoluted plot, it turned a mystery into a tragedy. However, this was the presentation, and, though it runs still, we must appraise it scene by scene, performer or puppet.

There is no doubt the concept was sound, and even the planning good. The Richards' Report in 1972 was an excellent synopsis. As the first draft of a final act it needed honing and tightening, but then the badger grinned for the first time. In his inimitable way he appeared in the gloom from nowhere, scratched himself, and shambled off drawing the crowd. On what is it a comment that some abandoned their study and followed in pursuit? The badger might have appeared as a sign but as a guide he got trampled underfoot.

As we have seen, the badger had a walk-on part back in the fifties in Switzerland, so had deer, affected by the same disease. The appearance of the badger in Britain did not in fact take place for another fifteen years; and only then did it become a star.

As work began to investigate the significance of Badger #1, found in Gloucestershire in April 1971 and declared positive for bovine TB in June, the Richards' committee – working in west Cornwall – while acknowledging the discovery, wisely confined themselves to Cornish evidence when they reported a year later. Only a late footnote implicated the badger:

On 27th June 1972 subsequent to the completion of the report, tubercle bacilli were isolated from badger faeces in West Penwith...

Again the badger was engaged and from this point it seemed to many as though it would run and run.

The first MAFF annual report stated:

Following the discovery of infection in badgers it has become Ministry policy to investigate the health status of badgers...

Appendix 2 of the same report shows that they investigated 4,468 badger samples (including 1,934 whole carcasses) compared to a total of 1,344 from all other species (an average of 56). Some species were represented by a single specimen; and of deer, already implicated in Switzerland, only four of unstated species were examined. Apart from badgers, infection was also found in three of 126 foxes, five of 163 rats, and two of 59 moles. With the help of Dr Paul Barrow's guide to sampling (see also Chapter 5), it is obvious that many of the sample sizes were irrelevant.

In January 1975, MAFF devised experiments at the Central Veterinary Laboratory (CVL), Weybridge designed to prove the 'virulence for calves of tubercle bacilli isolated from badgers', and the cross-transmission of the bacilli from badgers to cattle under controlled conditions. The result of the first experiment, published as a letter to *The Veterinary Record* on 14 June 1975, led David Coffey to suspect that 'the subtle soup of *Mycobacterium bovis* injected intravenously was of such a density that infection was almost guaranteed'. Other wildlife isolates were not used.

It was late 1982, four years after the experiments ended, before details of the experiment to show cross-transmission of the bacilli from badgers to cattle under controlled conditions were rather reluctantly, it seemed, published in the scientific press. Only brief in-progress accounts having appeared in early MAFF reports. The results were inconclusive, and really only showed that badgers artificially infected with large doses of the bacilli may become chronically ill and die, and that calves kept in the same communal stalls may also become infected.

The data were more interesting than the conclusions. It was poor work, and the findings were carelessly presented, and yet this work has become a central tenet. Similar experiments were not repeated with other susceptible species such as rats, deer, cats, dogs, moles, voles, mink and hedgehogs, and again there were no adequate controls. In the first experiment, three groups of badgers – presumed 'clean', although there is supposed to be no good diagnostic live-test (if there was, there would be no need to kill thousands of healthy badgers at all) – were housed in stalls about the size of a single garage. One badger from each group (of 3, 3 and 2) was inoculated with *M. bovis* at different strengths (as in the first experiment above), and the progression in them and their companions monitored.

In the second experiment, nine then ten badgers, trapped on a farm with a bad history of breakdowns, were housed in a covered yard 12 x 8.5m (though in fig 1 (7b) – from another paper – it is half that size) with some calves and again the course of the disease was monitored by clinical, immunological and bacteriological means. Over a period of up to four years in these cramped and stressful conditions, three of the badgers remained 'in very good condition', one in particular – D18 – a male, lived for 1305 days actually increasing its weight following the first isolation of *M. bovis* from its faeces (obviously, therefore, it had been infected for longer) before being killed at the end of the experiment. This badger's remarkable survival story is not discussed in the report.

Among the calves, despite the utterly unnatural, confined and contaminated conditions, in close quarters with a disproportionate number of infectious badgers, calves took at least six months before developing sensitivity to bovine tuberculin, and one took ten months. Though these findings obviously surprised MAFF, they managed to conclude:

The experiments...further demonstrate the *potential* of the badger population to become endemically infected and to act as a source of infection for cattle [my italics].

If 'potential' was all we were after, there had scarcely been any need to go to such lengths. Nevertheless, this conclusion still comes as something of a surprise after comments earlier in the *Discussion* part of the paper.

In the field the relative risk of cattle acquiring infection from badgers is low and usually only small numbers of cattle become infected. In these experiments the conditions were highly artificial but again the risk appeared to be low. Calves would regularly exist in the environment for up to five months without acquiring infection even though badgers were demonstrated to be excreting infected faeces during this period. The badgers made latrines in the cattle areas in both experiments but these were left undisturbed by the cattle.

The authors acknowledged

The experiments presented a number of problems. The badger is not a recognised laboratory animal... and the badgers used in these experiments made great efforts to escape... Thus it was necessary to hold them in concrete lined yards [with a door faced with a steel sheet].

The badgers were evidently highly stressed at times, and the authors admit that

Tuberculosis is a disease which may be aggravated by the stress of captivity and this may have shortened the badgers' lives.

Concerning the badger's ability to withstand such extreme artificial and stressful conditions while also endeavouring to cope with TB, it is merely stated that

One badger survived for three-and-a-half years after *M. bovis* was first isolated from its faeces, two badgers survived over two years and three badgers for over one year.

Disregarding for the moment that this contradicts the graphic and tabular presentation (see figs 7a and 7b), 'survived' is inappropriate because five out of six of these badgers seem to have been killed prematurely by the experimentors (one, D19, died under anaesthesia) and may well have 'survived' considerably longer.

The authors even confirm that 'examination of badger faeces samples provide a possible alternative to post-mortem examination to monitor the extent of *M. bovis* infection in badger populations'. MAFF have never been prepared to accept this humane test as diagnostic because of cases such as D21 which died with 'very extensive' lesions without having showed evidence of infection in the faeces. However, extensive sampling of this kind would probably provide enough data to help tip the scales in favour of a gradual decline. It would certainly ensure that immune groups were not removed as they have been in the *blitzkrieg* approach.

Before discussing the immunity aspect, there are other points arising out of the CVL experiments and their interpretation. The first concerns the evidence concentrated from Gloucestershire, and its questionable extrapolation to other regions where badgers seem much more resistant to TB. The second concerns the fate of badger D20 which was found 'badly decomposed...buried in a pile of moist hay and straw'. Although claimed 'it could not have been dead for more than a few days', elsewhere it is said not to have been seen 'for four days and after an extensive search of the accommodation (all 30 odd sq m of it) it was found decomposing under a heap of hay'. Quite apart from the lax husbandry (which would earn any zoo-keeper immediate dismissal), incidentally making one wonder about the overall control, there is a curious inconsistency here. If we are to believe that this badger after four days had 'putrid tissue' from which the bacilli could not be cultured, then we must assume it died in the summer. Fig 2 in the paper shows it dying in February 1977 but table 4 gives 837 days as its survival time following the first isolation of *M. bovis* from its faeces (in June or July 1975 according to fig 2); if table 4 is correct it would seem that D20 died in September or October 1977. This, of course, assumes that fig 2 is accurate for the first date, which can by no means be guaranteed because it would appear to be wrong in this respect for both D31 and D33 (*cf* table 4).

Such carelessness suggests hurried work – certainly lax refereeing – but since it took four years to appear this is unlikely; one is left with the suspicion that despite the great store set by it, MAFF actually bothered little with this piece of work. The die had been cast long before the CVL work had reached any kind of tenable conclusion. A lecturer in biology at a VI Form college examining the work recently said 'I wouldn't give an O-level student of mine any marks for it'. This work needs critical appraisal because it reveals much about MAFF's doctrine on this subject. All other evidence against the badger is circumstantial or associational. The question is not 'Is the badger involved in the epidemiology of TB in cattle?' but 'What is the role, how great the involvement, and what is the appropriate action?' We must also search for other factors, just as the Richards' team suggested in 1972, and we *must* enquire into what happened during the twenty years that preceded it.

Are we to assume that as infected cattle were gradually weeded out thanks to the Attested Herds Scheme, the prevalence in badgers followed this decline? If so, as seems reasonable, it suggests that diseased badgers are, to a large extent, an effect rather than a cause, and that the prevalence is higher in the south-west than elsewhere due to some other factor or factors. A higher than average density of badgers *and* cattle might be just one.

Studies into the epidemiology of bovine TB in cattle, badgers and other wildlife, mentioned in Chapter 5, endeavoured to be far less

---

Fig 7a (p.87) & *7b* (p.88) Summary of observations made on badgers naturally infected with *Mycobacterium bovis* at MAFF's

Central Veterinary Laboratory as published in *The Veterinary Record* of December 11, 1982. (*Reproduced by courtesy of The Veterinary Record*)

Fig 7a

TABLE 4: Summary of the observations made on the naturally infected badgers

Number	Sex	Weight on arrival (kg)	Weight at post mortem (kg)	Complement fixation test titre on arrival (reciprocal)	Peak complement fixation test titre recorded (reciprocal)	Survival time (days) from isolation of M bovis to death	Killed (K) or died (D)	Post mortem findings
D13	M	10·9	9·0	20	80	167	K	Tuberculous lesions in lungs and kidney. Purulent wound on rump from which M bovis was isolated twice during last three months of life
D16	F	9·1	8·4	—	20	335	D	Extensive tuberculosis of lungs, massive pleural exudate full of tubercle bacilli. Pleural surface of diaphragm covered in lesions
D17	F	11·8	10·7	10	160	165	D	Tuberculous lesions in lungs and liver. Minor lesions in kidneys
D18	M	10·9	11·3	20	160	1305	K	Tuberculous lesions in lungs and kidneys
D19	F	12·2	11·3	80	160	NI	D	Good bodily condition. Enlarged lymph nodes (anaesthetic death)
D20	M	8·2	10·0	—	80	837	D	Carcase badly decomposed
D21	M	10·0	7·7	—	160	NI	D	Very extensive tuberculosis of lungs and kidneys
D22	F	10·7	10·2	160	160	364	D	Tuberculous lesions in lungs and kidneys
D23	F	8·8	10·9	10	40	973	K	Small number of tuberculous lesions in lungs
D29	F cub	5·0	8·2	20	160	NI	D	Tuberculous lesions in lungs, liver and kidneys
D30	F cub	2·7	6·8	20	640	NI	D	Extensive tuberculous lesions in lungs and kidneys. M bovis isolated from urine
D31	M cub	4·8	12·7	—	160	372	K	Extensive tuberculous lesions in lungs and kidneys. M bovis isolated from urine
D33	F cub	4·1	12·2	40	160	372	K	Extensive tuberculous lesions in lungs and kidneys

NI No isolation

Fig 7b

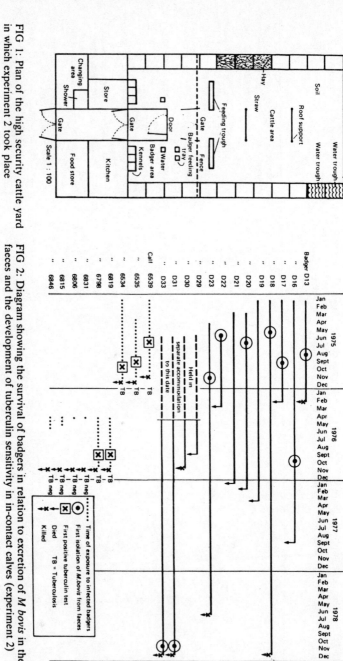

FIG 1: Plan of the high security cattle yard in which experiment 2 took place

FIG 2: Diagram showing the survival of badgers in relation to excretion of *M bovis* in their faeces and the development of tuberculin sensitivity in in-contact calves (experiment 2)

selective. Both set out to examine as much wildlife as possible but the bias in favour of easily caught species is plain.

One work by Barrow (for the NCC) and Gallagher (for MAFF) looked at wild animal populations in two parts of the Cotswold Hills. The samples obtained cannot represent relative densities: over the two areas 56 badgers were captured – more than any other warm-blooded species apart from the long-tailed field mouse (68). Otherwise, only 32 voles (of two species), 30 rats, 20 grey squirrels, 17 moles, 17 rabbits, 12 foxes, 10 shrews (of at least two species), 7 house mice and 5 weasels and *no* stoats or hedgehogs were taken nor deer of any kind; we are not told whether deer occurred on the farms or not.

One *must* take into account the relative population densities of these different species: moles, for example, can occur at up to 1,600/sq km compared to badgers at a maximum of only 20/sq km. Moles, rats, voles and deer are all known to be susceptible to TB. The authors state that the entire badger population was removed (i.e. 100% sample), I wonder what the percentage sample was of the other populations surveyed (an average of 18 from 12 other species). With regard to arthropod ectoparasites, 360 badger fleas and lice (+ 1 tick) were examined compared to a total of 105 from all other sources.

The work was obviously hampered by operational problems but the resultant bias was unfortunate and could have been misleading. Though acknowledging the shortcomings and stressing that the results should not be extrapolated to other situations, the authors felt their results were sufficiently comprehensive to believe that 'in the areas studied, the badger is the only species infected'. Would the results have been the same with a 100% sample of *all* other species?

Mosquitoes have been suggested in New Zealand as a possible vector but the sampling in Gloucestershire in the spring and November of 1979 precluded a mosquito sample. Other passive vectors could be flies; while scavenging birds such as crows not only feed on dead carcasses but also pasture and have been known to peck at open lesions on cattle. Magpies, in particular, have undergone a population explosion over much of the country in recent years.

Similar work carried out exclusively by MAFF centred at a farm near Kimmeridge Bay in Dorset which had seen 626 cattle slaughtered in the seventies, either because they were infected or in contact. The three papers which resulted were published in the same scientific journal (*Journal of Hygiene*) and though they were submitted after the appearance of Barrow and Gallagher's, make no reference to it.

This work covering events in the mid-seventies attempted to be more comprehensive. Thirty-three badgers were live-trapped and sent to Weybridge where they were used in the transmission experiments already discussed.

Following the Wild Creatures and Wild Plants Act 1975 which

reallowed the gassing of badgers, it was decided to eradicate badgers from the 'control area' of 1,200 hectares; this involved 196 sets.

As there was an abundance of other wild mammals in the area, it was decided to examine some to determine whether they also were infected with tuberculosis; the statement is hardly galvanised with zeal.

A total of 380 specimens were collected of 18 species (an average of about 21 per species compared to 18 in the earlier work). At the upper end of the individual totals, 90 rats were examined (*M. bovis* was isolated from two on culture), 73 voles, 57 rabbits, 39 wood mice and 27 squirrels; at the lower end, 9 weasels, 7 stoats, 7 foxes (one was positive on culture), 7 hares, 3 shrews, 3 hedgehogs, 2 mink and 9 deer of 3 species.

Again deer were neglected – all nine coming from a cull undertaken by the army on the extreme eastern edge of the control area two and half kilometres away from the focus of diseased badgers. The report is contradictory saying that roe deer (and much other wildlife) 'could be found over the entire area' with sika and some fallow deer to the west (nearer the focus), but ends by saying 'The population of wide-ranging species such as deer was low...and the sample is considered to be sufficiently large and representative'. The authors admit the difficulty of estimating population sizes but nevertheless conclude that a high proportion of most small mammals was caught – this is highly questionable. In making their assessments no account is taken of density variations in the different species or their ecology. It is admitted that 'moles were most active on the farmland' and yet only 33 were sampled. The only hedgehogs sampled were from fields near the sea. All this is understandable but nowhere is the bias towards easily captured mammals discussed.

When we look at the domestic animals investigated, MAFF shows positive discrimination. Although both dogs and cats are highly susceptible to TB, and although '(a) number of semi-wild cats lived around the farm buildings' only three 'were made available for examination... A number of dogs were accidentally live-trapped...but all were released and no dogs were examined'. Thus is scientific objectivity endangered.

Subjective analysis of this kind may often be unavoidable but bias, where it exists, should at least be acknowledged so that the reader may compensate; we must also look at the incentives which foster it. There is no doubt that these originated during the search for the 'missing link' back at the turn of the sixties. Was it inevitable that the badger would come to be seen as the sole link rather than one of several smaller ones? The prophecy began to self-fulfill.

Despite the Richards' Report, the case against the badger snowballed to such an extent that bovine TB and badgers became almost mutually inclusive. All that was left was to prove it.

Fig 8 Decision-making loop
expanded to show input of lobbying variables.

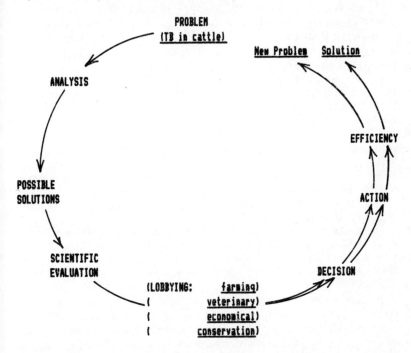

It is healthy to be suspicious of government scientists; no-one can pretend that politics and impartial enquiry are natural bed-fellows. Civil servants of integrity are inevitably going to find their principles compromised. Where this impinges on scientific liberty and begins to subvert the quest for truth it is not only intolerable but dangerous.

The public has been subjected,

said David Coffey in 1977,

to a campaign of fear recently in an attempt to engender a responsible attitude to our policy of animal quarantine and to kindle concern to prevent rabies entering Britain. One would feel more sanguine about our ability to deal with such an unfortunate contingency if one believed the state veterinary service were capable of examining the complex problem of transmission of disease between the natural fauna and our domestic stock without prejudice, using scientific methodology and without pandering to political restrictions imposed by their administrative masters.

Again in 1981, he said

if scientists are going to be allowed to be manipulated by bureaucrats for political expediency, the dangers for society are enormous.

Political judgements bedevil this programme. Consider its components: animal welfare, conservation and the mass killing of much loved and protected species, farmers' incomes, land use, disease control, the power to manage, prolonged and heavy government expenditure.

In Derek Pout's 1981 overlooked *Veterinary Record* article, he was appalled at the idea that official policy of the Ministry of Agriculture can be so stultifying to genuine enquiry and professional objectivity.

In part this is to be expected in a profession which has become subservient to the demands of the public to manipulate animals for their use. At the same time the profession is asked to arbitrate on matters of animal welfare, and it is doubtful if this duality is sustainable...

In a personal letter of 1985, Dr Pout writes

the essential element for everyone to remember is that unless one has control over the disposition of each and every badger, the control of the disease cannot be achieved in the same way as with cattle. There is intense political will within MAFF to succeed at any cost, because by acknowledging a change in attitude they believe they will have lost their authority to be custodians of animal health (especially in crises, i.e. rabies).

There is a further problem for the veterinary profession in that they only exist by virtue of the legal fact that animals are owned as property... Thus there are several persons in the profession who identify their survival with that of the small dairy farmer, and there are good historical and philosophical reasons for this position.

By now, too many badgers and cattle have died and too much money spent for a more enlightened solution to be welcomed. If the killing of badgers is stopped, it will be on economic grounds – that is the language of today – and it will enable many faces to be saved. These faces should have been saved long ago by fresh ones with newer ideas. It has to be wrong for persons in position of power to become personally ensnared in a controversy as sensitive and eclectic as this.

In a way, its very complexity is the problem. It is not a simple 'fire-brigade' matter. As we have seen, it involves scientific, economic, agricultural, legal and moral questions. Yet the administrative vets, beneath a supreme politician, hold sway. The hierarchy is such that biologists and ecologists – from whom we expect 20/20 vision – are governed by a vested sectional interest. Veterinary surgeons are as well equipped as anyone to begin to look at the problem but their vision must be tested first. Unfortunately, Research and Development is only the fourth MAFF priority (fifth, if it is true as one civil servant told me, that their paramount duty is to save the minister from any possible embarrassment).

The face of the ministry is at its feet. The pest control operatives who actually visit farmers and landowners, and are seen killing badgers by the public, are mostly unskilled, employed on low salaries, and come from the ranks of unemployed farm-workers. Some are conscientious and believe in what they are doing, some hate the job, and others regard it as a skive. If there is a job there at all (and this is discussed in the final chapter), it is one for trained scientific field officers. Though constrained by their strange priorities, it does not become the ministry to be seen as shadowy, furtive and inarticulate while highly trained and intelligent staff are gagged in public and subjected to all sorts of political constraints.

The good will that exists in abundance within MAFF must see the light of day. A course of frank discussion and open scientific debate would purge the beast. The unrealistic statutory requirement to eradicate TB, with which they are lumbered, should be replaced by a less absolute one. We could then all take stock and reflect; and some of the millions of pounds spent each year on killing mostly healthy badgers could be diverted into progressive research more in tune with the overture to the 21st opus.

Will some farmers be satisfied with anything less than the scalp of the badger now that it has been sold to them as the villain for so long? A few will not; the nervous and the insecure will thrash about blindly; the self-opinionated may carry on wreaking his vengeance and warming his cold heart on the blood of innocents. Most will want the truth.

If agriculture, from time to time, encounters an inexplicable phenomenon, maybe that is the price we all have to pay for attempting to dominate nature. Until we can resolve the problem one way or another, either by learning to live with nature in her fecund diversity or by reducing disease prevalence to a residual level everywhere, the taxpayer must compensate properly and fully the farmer who has done all that could reasonably be expected of him.

But there *are* farmers who abuse their stock and their land, who defy common-sense, who challenge nature, and who grasp at maximum profits. Many will be ignorant of the basis of their own prejudices, and must be educated. If some are in contempt of society, they hardly deserve to be propped up by it, and we should not be so nervous that we dare not say this. For cannot farmers be appraised like any other? Cannot the large and the rich help the small and the poor; cannot the ruthless sponsor the caring? From where did the land originally come? Is it the birthright of some and not others? Cannot we assess farmers by other standards: by sanity, moderation and balance, by care of stock and soil and of the environment, and with eyes able to see a distant prospect – so that the honourable can be acknowledged?

Now, in the realisation that we must give back to the land some of that which has been taken from it, the mania for profit, which was turning farming from the age-old harnessing of growth into a tyranny, shows signs of abating.

The simple badger is just a sign – how we regard it and respond to it will amplify much about our own condition.

ELEVEN

The Badger – Symbol or Slogan

Till kicked and torn and beaten out he lies
And leaves his hold and cackles groans and dies

(Clare)

The blaze of the badger flashes as he climbs out of the black earth-fastness into the twilight. It is a sign that has gone out all over Europe and Asia every night for three million years. How do we, the juvenile delinquents of this planet, gauge it? When I was measuring this problem, I made some notes; how do they look now – 40,000 words later? Has my own meagre analysis and the many months that preceded its preparation altered my perception?

Scribbled notes before, now deciphered ask: how does one evaluate without understanding, and judge without knowing? Do we protect rare life-forms for their sakes or for ours? Is any arbitrary valuation of ours a real measure of existence or a notional one? Because neither a scientist nor an economist has yet been able to express spiritual and philosophical values does not mean they do not exist. Is natural tactuality a flesh and blood indication of the intangible?

Should the badger be regarded as a symbol of something irreplaceable and of inestimable value – reaching back into the primeval purity of a world untainted by consciousness – or just an outdated and quaint relic – a nuisance and a hindrance; a grubby menace to the laundered fields?

A gamekeeper, no less, writing in 1985 said:

I would not dream of touching a badger no matter what he did; he was an English country gentleman before the Normans landed and he has a right to his place.

Gradually we find ourselves deeper and deeper in the briar patch of conservation – ensnared on the thorns, the vision impaired. Looking after the planet cannot compete with man's social or acquisitive desires. Though it is little more than enlightened commonsense, its credibility in a self-obsessed society is tenuous and endangered.

The debate that rages now around the hapless badger is about as even-handed as a fiddler crab. To avoid the charge of bias, as veterinary surgeon Robert W Howard expressly set out to do in his book *Badgers Without Bias* (1981), it seems as if we must accept at face value all state proclamations. I have tried not to do that. But the bias exists because we are human. Nobody in a position of power over other life-forms – which is everybody – can ask them what they think. If they do nothing else, the animal rights' activists remind us of this. It seems hypocritical to claim, as have the agricultural establishment and Lord Zuckerman, that concern for the badger is highly subjective.

The animals society depends on, seem to get a pretty raw deal when, living, they have served their usefulness. Do they not touch the grass and smell the slaughterhouse? A kinder life and a less brutal death might accrue from farms which were both less intensive and extensive. Drugs given by a compassionate hand with a favourite food in a familiar place might one sunny day countermand the push down death-row. If I were speaking of my grandmother rather than a cow, it would not be sentimental – it would be murder. Our lives are beset with bias.

So, if we speak of subjectivity, let's own up: our horses, dogs and cats we esteem more highly than the living stock of commerce.

Free species survive where they can – free but precarious. Those who adopt them would claim they cannot be subject to the same scale of judgement. If we are being honest, wildlife, for better or worse, represents a thing apart. Though it lives now in the shadow of man and has to take what he offers, it clings like an aborigine to a life more pristine than machine. But in that they live to give milk, and die to give meat, the living machines of man have a finite value of sorts. Society would find it more comfortable if they did not live, if they would go to 'market' quietly. It is only life that suffers to be abused and struck and goaded as it goes to be recycled.

We have turned a cycle. The badger survives precariously in over-crowded Britain. All things considered, he is an innocent; he hides himself away all livelong day but digs his holes at night, pushing out an apron of earth. The footpad Brock then trespasses on man's domain but traces his life through sightless scent, uncomprehending of the signs he leaves to the witness of a stark dawn. He can be a nuisance surely but threatens not even the thug who goads him.

The tubercle bacillus is the villain if you must; the badger can be its victim too. They are not able to *spread* it from one region of the country to another unless they are caught in traps and translocated. Some are caught in MAFF traps and sold to baiters – who have done for 'their own' – on the blackest market you could find in rural Britain.

The Ministry of Agriculture believes there to be no endemic low-level spread of the bacilli throughout the country but that it exists in pockets. Does this mean badgers are unable to spread it or are not given the chance to? If we accept that, with the high incidence in cattle during the first half of this century, a correspondingly high level of environmental contamination existed, it cannot be new to them.

So, what constitutes a pocket? The historic pattern is considered irrelevant, yet an enlightened response today demands to know whether, before interference, the 'pockets' were self-limiting, shrinking or extending 'naturally'. Maybe badgers are no more nor less likely to spread the disease than the pest officer who plods or drives from farm to farm actively seeking it.

If the badger and all other alien life-forms are to be vanquished by human dominion – sacrificed on some altar of avarice if they so much as look man in the eye – then no-one must be surprised if, as more and more recede, the less avaricious shout more and more loudly. When reason and logic fail, frustration sets in. And if the badger becomes a slogan, some sort of British panda, it won't be entirely its fault.

And it won't disturb the lie of the bones of all the badgers that have died, not through some natural cycle or disease or predator-prey relationship, but simply because they got in our way, or it was thought likely that at some time in the future they might conceivably get in our way.

Should we *automatically* expunge that which gets in our way or troubles our prosperity? Should, indeed, we be expected to be bought off with money for not wilfully destroying our origins? I am unhappy about this ransoming of the countryside. We must pay, but each in his own way, for the world we have inherited and that which we have borrowed from our children.

Bovine TB is a specialist problem of which the badger is an indicator. Are we killing the messenger? Agriculture was able to control the problem after the war by internal measures; nothing has changed. If it is found that some badgers in some parts of the country are a serious and irreconcilable threat, then those precise ones will have to go. It is up to the agriculture ministry to identify its target and solve its problem in a way that does not ride roughshod over the rights of others. In this they have everyone's support.

Let's be more precise ourselves: if there is a problem with badgers, or anything else for that matter, obstructing legitimate civilisation – and this is not a word to appropriate lightly – that cannot be allowed. Few would argue with the rights of an affronted poultry keeper to guard his stock from a rogue with an unnatural predilection, and if this means killing the offender then, providing it is done considerately, humanely and with reverence, so be it.

What is going on now, in the killing fields of Britain, is none of these things. It is, for whatever reason, an over-reaction and an overkill; perhaps it is a comment on our own inadequacy. Yet there is another way of approaching this occasion.

For some years, Dr John Stanford, an immunologist at the Middlesex Hospital's School of Pathology, has been working on a potential oral vaccine against tuberculosis for badgers. Much of what follows is taken from a summary of the work very kindly given me by Dr Stanford and his assistant Dr Kahlid Mahmood – for whom we have to thank Iraq and the Iraqi government.

Fig 9 Early results of Dr John Stanford's work at the Middlesex Hospital's School of Pathology which demonstrates the possibilities of protecting badgers from tuberculosis by BCG vaccine.

SOME EXPERIMENTAL DATA ILLUSTRATED

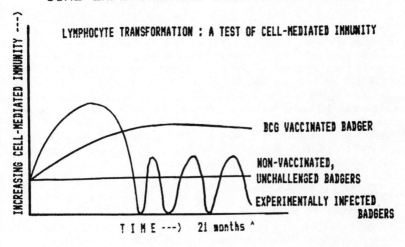

LYMPHOCYTE TRANSFORMATION : A TEST OF CELL-MEDIATED IMMUNITY

INCREASING CELL-MEDIATED IMMUNITY --->

BCG VACCINATED BADGER

NON-VACCINATED, UNCHALLENGED BADGERS

EXPERIMENTALLY INFECTED BADGERS

T I M E ---> 21 months ^

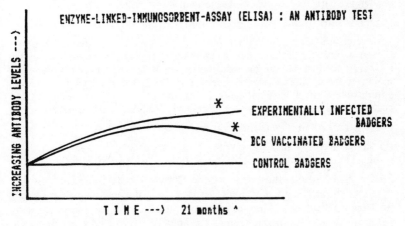

ENZYME-LINKED-IMMUNOSORBENT-ASSAY (ELISA) : AN ANTIBODY TEST

INCREASING ANTIBODY LEVELS --->

* EXPERIMENTALLY INFECTED BADGERS

* BCG VACCINATED BADGERS

CONTROL BADGERS

T I M E ---> 21 months ^

* ANTIBODIES OF DIFFERENT SPECIFICITIES

Dr Stanford is a member of MAFF's Consultative Panel but he and Dr Mahmood feel obliged to begin their account by saying:

The present policy of the Ministry of Agriculture to eliminate, or at least control tuberculosis in badgers has been less successful than was hoped, perhaps even disastrous. As an adjunct to these activities, and hopefully as an alternative if successful, we have been working on the immunology of badgers with a special interest in developing a successful vaccine...

Apart from Iraq, they also received financial assistance from their own department, considerable help in holding live badgers as well as collaboration with some of the work, of MAFF staff at CVL.

The experimental plan was, in principle,

to apply technology developed in human medicine to the badger's problem. First...a number of immunological techniques for assessing progress of infection and vaccine efficacy in badgers [had to be established]. The three tests we have used are skin tests, lymphocyte transformation [see Chapter 2], and enzyme linked immunosorbent assay (ELISA) [see note on p.99]. With these tests we have followed the course of changes, with time, in control animals, the development of immunity in BCG vaccinated animals and the course of immune perturbation in animals experimentally infected with bovine tubercle bacilli. In our second series of experiments, control animals and BCG vaccinated animals have been challenged with virulent tubercle bacilli. If BCG prevents badgers from developing tuberculosis, modifies it to an indolent and much less infectious form, or significantly delays its onset then vaccination works and the third phase of our studies can begin. This will be the development of a suitable oral vaccine.

The results have shown

differences in all three types of test between control, vaccinated, and infected badgers [see fig 9]. Preliminary evidence from the BCG vaccinated animals challenged with tubercle bacilli suggests at least some protective effect...

Drs Stanford and Mahmood comment that there are

parameters for assessing vaccine efficacy and hopefully evidence for some success with BCG. The next step is to try live BCG given by mouth (this works in man) and then suspensions of a variety of killed mycobacteria given by mouth. In theory, if BCG works, then it should be possible to develop an orally administered killed vaccine. Only a vaccine of this type is likely to be acceptable, cheap to make and relatively easy to administer in pellets.

Dr Stanford in a personal communication says that

such a cold account can hardly give any idea of the excitement we have over the results. I am now in little doubt that a vaccine can be developed for the badger.

However, he admits that a lot more work needs to be done. He feels the ministry should be encouraged to extend their studies in epidemiology, and try to find out why badger communities in certain areas are susceptible to TB. In one letter, Dr Stanford has identified the dual clinical problem and pointed the way to creative science. I do not feel though that the political pressures put upon MAFF, and the bureaucracy of CVL administration are conducive to this.

Opposition to these experiments on philosophical grounds are quite legitimate. I feel, for what it's worth, that the animals here are doomed anyway and that the work may help to save hundreds more, maybe thousands. I know they are loved and respected by the workers, and I feel that the sacrifice we impose upon them is better than a bullet at dawn.

The work confirms that some badgers though susceptible to tubercle bacilli when injected into them, as happens with a bite wound, are resistant as a species. This is quite different from the possums in New Zealand – which seem to have little resistance. Stanford points out that when dealing with a disease resistant species, especially one living in small colonies like the badger, a vaccine reducing the number of susceptible animals by 50% will result in many communities containing *no* susceptible individuals. Thus, progressively, the disease should disappear as tuberculous and susceptible individuals, and the chances of their meeting are both reduced. To achieve the same success with possums, a vaccine producing over 90% protection would be needed. These are crucially important details.

Nature, if left alone, might do all this work for us. TB once recorded from voles now appears to have disappeared. Is this relevant? No-one knows. In MAFF's own no-interference study area, badgers appear able to contain the disease themselves and are less a threat to cattle than outside where they are subjected to inept blitzes.

My wish is that mankind takes note of such critical touchstones as the badger – created, refined and perfected since the Pliocene – and sees in them strategies for his own survival and development, recent as it is.

'*We are an enduring lot, and we may move out for a time, but we wait, and are patient, and back we come. And so it will ever be,*' said Badger.

(Kenneth Graham: *Wind in the Willows*)

N.B. ELISA (see p.98): blood serum from the test animal is added to a test tube which contains an antigen specific for *M. tuberculosis* antibodies. If the serum contains these antibodies (indicating the test animal was infected) they combine with the antigen in the test tube. On addition of an appropriate substrate, a coloured solution results if this antibody/antigen reaction has occurred. In a given time, the intensity of the colour produced (measured as the optical density) is related to the amount of antibody present.

APPENDIX I

The Comparative Tuberculin Test

This diagnostic test has been widely used in Britain as a means of discovering *Mycobacterium bovis* infection in cattle since 1935. It entails injecting 0.1 ml of bovine tuberculin (PPD – a purified protein derivative acquired from growing bovine tubercle bacilli in the laboratory) into the skin of cattle. If infected a localised response is set up which causes a thickening of the skin – most reliably assessed after three days in cattle; uninfected cattle show little or no response. In Britain, the sensitive neck skin is used which causes a high number of 'false-positives' (animals reacting which are found on post-mortem not to be infected with *M. bovis*); in America, which began its eradication campaign in 1917, the skin near the tail is used, and this significantly reduces the number of false-positives.

If the thickness of the fold of skin, measured with callipers, has increased by more than 3 mm the animal is classed as a 'reactor'. The false-positives may have reacted to a closely-related harmless mycobacteria, and in order to reduce this incidence, cattle are also injected with avian tuberculin, and the results compared. Cattle infected with other mycobacteria will react to avian tuberculin but those infected only with *M. bovis* will not. Those reactors which react to bovine tuberculin but not avian are slaughtered.

APPENDIX II

Official procedure following a herd breakdown (after Zuckerman 1980)

Routine tuberculin testing (see Appendix I) is generally carried out by local veterinary surgeons. MAFF officers become involved when a (doubtful) reactor is found. If post-mortem examination of a reactor reveals visible lesions of tuberculosis, MAFF tries to discover the source of infection and investigates:

The Reactor
1. The animal's history, with particular attention to its origin (home-bred or purchased); any veterinary treatment and whether it was alive during any previous outbreaks of tuberculosis on the farm.
2. The animal's movements on the farm since the last tuberculin tests.
3. Where there are a number of reactors, whether they were at any time in the same group.

Other Animals
4. The farm's tuberculosis history.
5. The history of contiguous premises.
6. The standard of fencing and details of straying onto or off the affected premises.
7. The use of fertilisers; access to slaughterhouses or knackeryard waste, including products used for feeding dogs; or whether raw milk products have been brought to the farm and could have been in contact with stock.
8. Recent purchases.
9. Recent sales and deaths of cattle including those consigned to a knackeryard.
10. The incidence of other cattle (e.g. hired bulls) on the farm or passing through it.
11. Goats present are tuberculin tested.
12. The history of disease in other species of animal on the farm especially pigs, cats and dogs.

Humans
13. Whether the farm adjoins a lay-by, caravan site or refuse tip.
14. The possibility of pasture or drinking water being contaminated by sewage or cesspool effluent.
15. The history of illness in the farmer, his family, employees and relief milkers.

Other Sources
16. Old buildings in recent use or those under alteration which might have been contaminated.
17. The location of any nearby slaughterhouses or knackeryards.

(*NB. If negative a PBI (Preliminary Badger Investigation) is now initiated*)

APPENDIX III

Contact Points

Badger Groups exist in most sensitive areas, and may be contacted through your local County Trust for Nature Conservation, the more members they have the more effective they can be in protecting local badgers and sets from increasing pressure. In the event of difficulty write to:

Royal Society for Nature
Conservation
The Green
Nettleham
LINCOLN LN2 2NR

The Badger Protection Society
15 Sanderstead Court Avenue
Sanderstead
Surrey

Other useful addresses:

Animal Aid
7 Castle Street
TONBRIDGE
Kent TN9 1BH

League Against Cruel Sports
Sparling House
83/87 Union Street
LONDON SE1 1SG

MAFF
Great Westminster House
Horseferry Road
LONDON SW1P 2AE

The Mammal Society
Burlington House
Piccadilly
LONDON W1V 0LR

Nature Conservancy Council
19/20 Belgrave Square
LONDON SW1X 8PY

World Wildlife Fund
Panda House
11–13 Ockford Road
GODALMING
Surrey GU7 1QU

APPENDIX IV

Principal References and Recommended Further Reading

Badger Working Group, 1984, 'Badgers, cattle & tuberculosis', *A Report to the Minister of Agriculture's Bovine Tuberculosis Review Group*, World Wildlife Fund-UK.

Barrow PA, 1982, 'Bovine Tuberculosis in the Badger – a fresh look', *Health and Hygiene*, **4**,2,3,4.

Barrow PA, 1982, 'Must badgers be destroyed?' *New Scientist*, 21 October.

Barrow PA, 1983, 'A note on a method to aid sampling populations for characteristics', *J. Applied Bacteriology*, **54**, 311–12.

Bouvier G, 1962, 'Observations sur les maladies du gibier, des oiseaux et des poissons', *Schweizer Arch. Tierheil*, **104**, 440–50.

Carwardine M, 1984, 'New outlook for badgers', *World Wildlife News*, WWF, Autumn.

Cheeseman CL, Jones GW, Gallagher J and Mallinson PJ, 1981, 'The population structure, density and prevalence of tuberculosis in badgers from four areas in south-west England', *J. Applied Ecology*, **18**, 794–804.

Cheeseman CL and Mallinson PJ, 1981, 'Behaviour of badgers infected with bovine tuberculosis', *J. Zoology*, **194**, 284–89.

Coffey D, 1977, 'Death to badgers?' *New Scientist*, 17 November.

Collins CH and Grange JM, 1983, A review. 'The bovine tubercle bacillus', *J. Applied Bacteriology*, **55**, 13–29.

Crittenden A, 1983, 'An account of badger digging', *RSPCA Today*, **43**, 9–11, 14.

Drabble P, 1979, *No badgers in my wood*, Michael Joseph.

Drabble P, 1981, 'Gassing badgers is wrong', *Observer*, 27 September.

Dunbar F, 1955, *Mind and body*, New York.

Evans H and Thompson HV, 1981, 'Bovine tuberculosis in cattle in Great Britain. Eradication of the disease from cattle and the role of the badger as a source of *M. bovis* for cattle', *Animal Regulation Studies*, **3**, 191–216.

Flowerdew JR, 1981, 'Badger controversy', *Nature,* **289**, 830–31.

Gallagher J and Nelson J, 1979, 'Cause of ill health and natural death in badgers in Gloucestershire', *Vet. Record,* **105**, 546–551.

Grange J. 1976, 'Enzymic breakdown of amino acids and related compounds by suspensions of washed mycobacteria', *J. Applied Bacteriology,* **41**, 425–431.

Grange JM, 1982, 'Koch's tubercle bacillus. A Centenary Reappraisal', *Zentralblatt fur Bakteriologie, Mikrobiologie, und Hygiene; I. Abt. Originale, A.,* **251**, 297–307.

Gwent Badger Group, 1978, *Briefly on badgers.*

Hardy P, 1975, *A lifetime of badgers,* David & Charles.

Harris S, 1984, 'The not-so-black-and-white-badger', *BBC Wildlife,* **2**, 9.

Howard RW, 1981, *Badgers without bias,* Abson Books, Bristol.

Inglis B, 1981, *The diseases of civilisation,* Hodder & Stoughton.

Kissen D, 1958, *Emotional factors in pulmonary tuberculosis,* London.

Kruuk H, 1978, 'Spatial organisation and territorial behaviour of the European badger', *J. Applied Ecology,* **184**, 1–19.

Kruuk H and Parish T, 1982, 'Factors affecting population density, group size and territory size of the European badger', *J. Zoology,* **196**, 31–39.

Kurten B, 1968, *Pleistocene mammals of Europe,* Weidenfeld & Nicholson.

Little TWA, Naylor PF and Wilesmith JW, 1982, 'Laboratory study of *M. bovis* infection in badgers and calves', *Vet. Record,* **111**, 550–57.

Little TWA, Swan C, Thompson HV and Wilesmith JW, 1982, 'Bovine Tuberculosis in domestic and wild mammals in an area of Dorset', I, II and III, *J. Hyg., Camb,* **89**, 195–234.

Macdonald DW, 1984, 'Badgers and bovine tuberculosis – case not proven', *New Scientist,* 25 October.

McDiarmid A, 1969, 'Diseases in free-living wild animals', *Symposia Zool. Soc. Ldn,* No. 24.

MAFF, 1972, *Inquiry into bovine tuberculosis in West Cornwall,* Richards (Chairman).

MAFF, 1976–85, *Bovine tuberculosis in badgers,* Annual Reports.

MAFF, 1983, *Bovine tuberculosis: a badger control manual and code of practice,* ADAS, December.

Neal E, 1948, *The badger,* Collins.

Neal E, 1977, *Badgers,* Blandford Press.

Overend E, 1980, *Badgers in trouble*, Trowbridge.

Pout DD, 1981, 'Tuberculosis in badgers', *Vet. Record*, 12 December, 541.

Pout DD, 1981, *An examination of the Zuckerman Report*, Unpubl. document.

Ratcliffe JE, 1983, *Through the badger gate*, Dalesman Books.

Snider WR, Cohen D, Reif D, Stein J and Prier JE, 1971, Tuberculosis in canine and feline populations, Study of high-risk populations in Pennsylvania, 1966–68, *Am. Rev. Res. Diseases*, **104**, 866–76.

Stanford JL and Mahmood KH, 1985, 'Summary of work on a potential oral vaccine against tuberculosis for badgers', Unpubl. document.

Walker P, 1981, 'Why we have to gas badgers', *Observer*, 17 January.

Zuckerman Lord, 1980, 'Badgers, cattle and tuberculosis', *Report to Rt Hon Peter Walker MP*, HMSO.

Zuckerman Lord, 1981, 'The badger and TB controversy', *Sunday Times*, 4 January.

Zuckerman Lord, 1981a, 'The great badger debate', *Nature*, **289**, 628–30.

APPENDIX V

A Note on the Natural History of the Badger

The European badger (*Meles meles*) is a member of the Mustelidae family of musk-bearing carnivores in the order Carnivora; its closest relatives, therefore, in Britain are other mustelids such as the otter, pine marten, stoat and weasel. It is the largest British representative: males on average weigh 12 kilograms (26lbs) and measure about 75cm (30 inches) long not counting the tail (15cm).

Though the badger occurs throughout Britain, it is most common in the hills of the south-west, and most rare in the flat agricultural deserts of East Anglia and high mountains. Elsewhere in Europe, it is widely distributed south of the Arctic Circle and is found across Asia, north of the Himalayas, as far east as China and Japan.

The badger is a stocky and immensely strong animal of grizzled appearance which is caused by a coat made up on the upper parts of guard-hairs which are individually whitish at the base and black towards the tip (underparts are virtually all black); the overall shade of the animal is governed by the proportions of this pattern – though it can also reflect the hue of the soil in which it burrows. Of most striking appearance is the strongly marked black and white striped head, which probably warns potential attackers of the badger's formidable bite, and also aids recognition between individuals as they meet on their scent-trails at night or in the gloom of their underground tunnels. Although badgers have no real enemies left in Britain apart from man and his machines, their cubs do, and Ernest Neal considers it significant that they assume these markings almost from birth. In order to dig its extensive subterranean sets, the badger needs to be powerfully built with strong forelegs finished off with long pick-like claws. The head is small, resulting in wedge-shaped forequarters, and the eyes and ears reduced. Nevertheless, hearing is acute though the principal sense is, without doubt, that of smell.

Just why the badger needs its ferocious bite is something of a mystery, for it feeds predominantly on earthworms, other invertebrates and plant material; larger animal food is usually scavenged. The lower jaw is articulated by great temporalis muscles attached anteriorly and posteriorly to the median sagittal crest (= interparietal ridge) which is so distinctive of the badger's skull. Because of the great leverage thus exerted the articulation has had to be modified to withstand the stresses incurred, and the badger's jaw cannot be dislocated except by breaking.

Maybe the badger, forced, certainly historically, to excavate its labyrinthine tunnels amongst tree-roots needed such equipment simply to clear tree roots. Sets are still usually excavated on sloping well-drained ground under cover of trees or shrubs, often in woodland; but scrubby sea-cliffs, overgrown quarries and mature hedgerows are also favourite places. Mounds of earth outside large holes (never less than 25cm in diameter), usually in groups, indicate a set. If the spoil is freshly turned over and shows evidence of clean bedding (bundles of leaves), and if growing vegetation is flattened or if flies are to be seen around the entrance, it indicates that badgers are in residence. Fresh dung in shallow pits can often be found nearby.

Cubs, two or three to a litter, are born early in the year after the blastocyst has lain dormant in the uterine cavity possibly for up to a year before becoming embedded; mating takes place at any time except deepest winter. This process is known as 'delayed implantation'. It allows mating to occur when badgers are in peak condition, in the summer and autumn, but ensures that cubs are born at the best time for them – with a full summer and autumn ahead of them in which to grow and develop before their first winter. Even so, about seventy-five per cent of badgers fail to survive this most testing time, usually due to insufficient reserves of fat.

APPENDIX VI

John Clare's full poem on the persecution of the badger and an additional sonnet on the taming of the badger (both reproduced in the original style)

The badger grunting on his woodland track
With shaggy hide and sharp nose scrowed with black
Roots in the bushes and the woods and makes
A great hugh burrow in the ferns and brakes
With nose on ground he runs a awkard pace
And anything will beat him in the race
The shepherds dog will run him to his den
Followed and hooted by the dogs and men
The woodman when the hunting comes about
Go round at night to stop the foxes out
And hurrying through the bushes ferns and brakes
Nor sees the many hol[e]s the badger makes
And often through the bushes to the chin
Breaks the old holes and tumbles headlong in

When midnight comes a host of dogs and men
Go out and track the badger to his den
And put a sack within the hole and lye
Till the old grunting badger passes bye
He comes and hears they let the strongest loose
The old fox hears the noise and drops the goose
The poacher shoots and hurrys from the cry
And the old hare half wounded buzzes bye
They get a forked stick to bear him down
And clapt the dogs and bore him to the town
And bait him all the day with many dogs
And laugh and shout and fright the scampering hogs
He runs along and bites at all he meets
They shout and hollo down the noisey streets

He turns about to face the loud uproar
And drives the rebels to their very doors
The frequent stone is hurled where ere they go

When badgers fight and every ones a foe
The dogs are clapt and urged to join the fray
The badger turns and drives them all away
Though scarcly half as big dimute and small
He fights with dogs for hours and beats them all
The heavy mastiff savage in the fray
Lies down and licks his feet and turns away
The bulldog knows his match and waxes cold
The badger grins and never leaves his hold
He drive[s] the crowd and follows at their heels
And bites them through the drunkard swears and reels

The frighted women takes the boys away
The blackguard laughs and hurrys on the fray
He tries to reach the woods a awkard race
But sticks and cudgels quickly stop the chace
He turns agen and drives the noisey crowd
And beats the many dogs in noises loud
He drives away away and beats them everyone
And then they loose them all and set them on
He falls as dead and kicked by boys and men
Then starts and grins and drives the crowd agen
Till kicked and torn and beaten out he lies
And leaves his hold and cackles groans and dies

Some keep a baited badger tame as hog
And tame him till he follows like the dog
They urge him on like dogs and show fair play
He beats and scarcely wounded goes away
Lapt up as if asleep he scorns to fly
And siezes any dog that ventures nigh
Clapt like a dog he never bites the men
But worrys dogs and hurrys to his den
They let him out and turn a harrow down
And there he fights the host of all the town
He licks the patting hand and trys to play
And never trys to bite or run away
And runs away from noise in hollow trees
Burnt by the boys to get a swarm of bees

(John Clare 1793-1864)

John Clare's badger poems by Eric Robinson

Like most of Clare's other poems about wild creatures other than birds – such poems as 'The Marten', 'The Fox', 'The Vixen', 'The Hedgehog' and 'The Mouse's Nest' – the two poems about the badger derive from Clare's Northborough period, 1832-37, and strongly reflect the turmoil of his mind at this time of removal, just before he went mad.

His uprooting from his native village of Helpston, though intended by the Fitzwilliam family as an act of kindness and at first greeted by Clare as a step towards the independence he always sought and never attained, led to a period of ill-health both for himself and his children, of increasing stress within his home and conflict with his wife, and of growing alienation from his rural neighbours. Clare lost his bearings and, in his usual way, spoke of not knowing which quarter the sun was in and of trees and plants being unrecognizable. He said that his new village had no old hollow oak trees, no old furze like Langley Bush, no familiar hiding places.

Clare began to feel himself more and more of an outsider, a victim both of his patronizing middle-class admirers and of his rural creditors, a failure in his new role as smallholder and a disaster as a family provider. To avoid the gaze of the curious, his new cottage was so built that its door did not face the street. He felt himself like Job, whose story he had learnt by heart as a child, a man betrayed by his friends, his neighbours and even by God. Many of the poems he wrote at this time are written in the guise of a looker-on, almost of a vagrant.

His poems about animals reflect his sense of abandonment and persecution, and none more strongly than 'The Badger' (i). In it, he does not *describe* the badger, he *is* the badger; a wild half-mad creature escaping from his hunters, running the gauntlet, hit by sticks and stones, showing a vicious sort of courage and indomitable will in the face of the village rabble. Every word of the poem breathes the raunchy stench of fear and no other poem in the English language equals it in this characteristic. The badger is an enduring and surviving beast broken down by superior strength and overwhelming nastiness:

Till kicked and beaten out he lies
And leaves his hold and cackles groans and dies

Because of Professor Kelsey Thornton's constant reminder to me of Clare's skill in bringing his poems to completion, I have at last recognized that this is the obvious ending of the poem and that the 14-line stanza (or sonnet) that appears on a separate piece of paper close to 'The Badger' in the same Peterborough manuscript is in fact a separate poem. This poem is about a *tame* badger. The animal retains some of his old courage but is now domesticated. Even the strange infelicity of lines 12 and 13 where the badger is said first never to run away and then, immediately, to run away *'from noise in hollow trees'* may be accounted for by saying that the tamed badger still retains some vestige of his wild state. It may be noted in passing that a hollow tree was to Clare a symbol of refuge and was usually an old hollow oak, the sort of tree that Northborough did not possess.

'The Badger', like other poems of the period is a sonnet-sequence, composed of end-stopped lines, each of which has been compared to a Bewick engraving in the completeness of the picture and the sharpness of the outline.

The old fox hears the noise and drops the goose
The poacher shoots and hurrys from the cry
And the old hare half wounded buzzes bye

Here each vignette is in sequence, like the woodcuts in Fenning's Spelling Book which Clare tells us he so much enjoyed as a boy. But look also at that powerful Chaucerian word 'buzzes' which excites both the auditory and visual senses almost like the cartoon of the Roadrunner. Everywhere in these poems the language is localised and familiar – 'scrowed', 'awkward', 'hols', 'cackles' – but it is not simply dialect. The word 'dimute', a diminutive form of 'diminutive' is Clare's own coinage and though the earlier reading of this word as 'demure' is wrong it may also suggest the way in which Clare sometimes telescopes words together. It stops us for a moment but then startles by its precision.

Clare reflects some of his age's anxiety about cruelty to animals but he is no sentimentalist. Part of his uniqueness is that he knows, like the badger, what it is to be a quarry (ii).

(i) Eric Robinson, *John Clare's Autobiographical Writings*, Oxford University Press, 1983, pp 14-15.

(ii) Those interested in Clare's poetry may consult E. Robinson and D. Powell, *Clare*, Oxford Authors Series, 1984.

(*Note from the author:* I am greatly indebted to Professor Robinson for contributing these lucid notes. The John Clare Society has been formed to bring together lovers of Clare and natural history. Enquiries to George Dixon, 8 Priory Road, Peterborough, Cambridgeshire.)

INDEX

(Major References Only Included)

(*Author's note*: The author wishes to thank John Martin for compiling the index.)